The LITTLE WASHER
of SORROWS

The LITTLE WASHER
of SORROWS

KATHERINE FAWCETT

thistledown press

Thistledown Press Ltd.
410 2nd Avenue North
Saskatoon, Saskatchewan, S7K 2C3
www.thistledownpress.com

Library and Archives Canada Cataloguing in Publication

Fawcett, Katherine, 1967–, author
The little washer of sorrows / Katherine Fawcett.
Short stories.
Issued in print and electronic formats.
ISBN 978-1-77187-049-8 (pbk.).–ISBN 978-1-77187-066-5 (html).–
ISBN 978-1-77187-067-2 (pdf)
I. Title.
PS8561.A942L58 2015   C813'.6   C2015-900481-0
C2015-900482-9

Cover and book design by Jackie Forrie
Printed and bound in Canada

creative
SASKATCHEWAN

Thistledown Press gratefully acknowledges the financial assistance of the Canada Council for the Arts, the Saskatchewan Arts Board, and the Government of Canada through the Canada Book Fund for its publishing program.

The LITTLE WASHER *of* SORROWS

This book is dedicated with love to my parents: Leslie and John Stoddart. I forgive you for not letting me and Kirst drive to Penticton for donuts with those guys we met camping in Naramata that time. Turns out you did not ruin my life after all.

CONTENTS

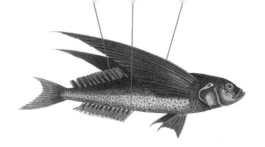

Captcha

THE DAY I DISCOVERED MY TRUE nature began like any other day: I woke up, gave Pete a blowjob, and went downstairs to fry up a pan of bacon.

It was June 14th. Ten degrees outside, with falling barometric pressure. There were periorbital dark circles under Pete's eyes when he came down in his blue dress shirt and yellow tie.

"Is it going to be another late one?" I asked. Pete's a busy tax accountant with H&R Block. "Because, don't forget, it's your poker night. I'll do wings and nachos. Unless you want me to call the boys and cancel. If you have too much work."

"No, it's good. I'm leaving at five tonight no matter what. I need the distraction." He scratched his genitals through his slacks. "You'd think people would learn."

I spread Skippy on his toast and filled his go-mug with coffee.

"I swear to God, Margo, the self-employed are the worst. They think they can just hand me a shoebox of crumpled receipts and boom, I'll magically figure it all out and get them a rebate by the next morning."

"Well, don't try and be a super-hero," I said. "You're only human."

Once he'd gone, I put a load of whites in the washing machine and started vacuuming. I had a part-time job as a marketing representative for Kokanee Beer. It was a good job, mostly at weekend festivals and sporting events. They provided a company van, and I was paid in Kokanee product and tickets to games and special events, which Pete and his friends enjoyed. I know that I was hired because I represent what men think of as a "good-time girl". My profile is as follows: I have long straight blonde hair, larger than average blue eyes, puffy lips, symmetrical facial features, and a forty-one-inch chest. I visit a tanning salon every forty-eight hours to maintain a bronzed glow. I have a masters' degree in applied mathematics, but my employer said that was irrelevant. I have no siblings. My parents died in a fiery plane crash when I was young. Pete and I have no children, as I am infertile. Essentially I have no living genetically related family. But I have Pete.

"Margo, why the hell did you study applied mathematics if you only want to sit on the back of a convertible in a bikini outside football games handing out beer while all those drunken bozos leer at you?" my mother-in-law once asked. Pete told her to shove it, but I replied truthfully: I use my mathematical education every day. It helps me make sense of the world.

My only other family is Pete's older brother Jordan, his wife Cara, and their two children. Whenever we get together, Pete offers me up to his brother in some way. "Go ahead, Jor," he said at the past Easter dinner. "Try it. Try and make her laugh. She's just not ticklish." Then my husband crossed his arms, leaned against the kitchen counter, and watched Jordon wiggle his fingers under my arms and poke between my ribs.

Captcha

Although Pete is not a licensed investment banker, he occasionally dabbles in the stock market. Jordan and Cara are fiscally illiterate, so several years ago they gave my husband full access to their bank account, in order for Pete to make investments on their behalf as he saw fit.

"See what you can do for us," said Jordon. "Make us rich." His and Cara's trust in Pete's financial judgement has thus far failed to turn a profit, but no one is overly anxious. "One day, bro," Pete says. "One day."

It was a Thursday, so after I put the whites in the drier, I started cleaning Pete's den-slash-office. I recycled papers, vacuumed the carpet, and set to polishing the desktop. I noticed a vehicle insurance renewal confirmation form on his bureau that needed to be refiled. Usually Pete keeps his filing cabinet locked, but he must have forgotten to close it completely, so I pulled the drawer open to refile the paper.

I flipped through the drawer — Marriage Certificate, Mortgage, Moving Expenses — until my fingers stopped on a file near the back that I had not noticed before. It was labelled neatly in ink: R9k4l. The numerical/alphabetical combination made no sense to me. I pulled the file out gently, making a mental note that it was tucked between Phone Bills and Receipts/Automotive so I could replace it in exactly the same spot.

Inside the R9k41 file was a glossy brochure and a small leather billfold. The brochure cover featured a photo of a smiling couple under the words *Cupid's Creation*. Below, it read: *True Love by Design*. I opened the brochure. There were more photos of smiling couples, some barely dressed, in various states of rapture.

At first I thought it was some kind of dating service. Why would Pete need the service of a date? What was missing from our marriage that he needed to arrange an extramarital liaison? It would be not only wildly out of character, but also quite careless of him, to put us both at risk of contracting a sexually transmitted disease.

On the second page I read: *Select from one of our prototypes or design your own model. Our team of advanced Mate Creation specialists guarantees that your dream partner will be exactly as you envision her/him/it. Your satisfaction is ensured by our lifetime, money-back guarantee.* Saliva was accumulating in my mouth.

I flipped to the back page: *Your robot comes complete with over 94% organic human organs, 6,500 gigabytes of artificial memory, variable preprogrammed knowledge, a capacity for genuine emotional and physical reactions, and the ability to form human bonds and integrate new knowledge on a real time basis.*

Was he seriously thinking of ordering a robotic sex toy? What kind of a man had I married? I thought I knew Pete. I thought we had no secrets from each other. And now this? Did he already have her? Was he keeping her somewhere? Was he with her right now? How much had this thing cost? What other perversions was he concealing?

I picked up the leather billfold but did not open it. The temperature in the room had risen two degrees in the past eight minutes, and the Okanagan sun shone at a seventy-six-degree angle through the horizontal slats. What if it held a receipt of some kind? Warranty papers? A delivery notice? If the object in my hand contained confirmation of this horror, I didn't want to see it — yet I had to know. Hands shaking, I unfolded the thin case and revealed two wallet-sized photos, both of me or someone who looked exactly like me. One was a close-up head-shot that could have been taken that very morning. The other, a full-sized nude photo.

A laminated card had been tucked into the inner pocket of the billfold beside the photos. In bold Harrington typeface was the title "Certificate of Authenticity" below which read:

Cupid's Creation
Serial Number: R9k4l

On the reverse side of the card was a detailed physical description of me, from my height and weight to my blood type, voice timbre, walking gait, and the third-power ellipsoidal formula describing the pattern of my fingerprints. And folded neatly in an inner pocket was a receipt. $250,000 cash, dated February 14, 2009. Our first date. My birthday.

It didn't make any sense. Was I perhaps a model for one of Cupid's Creations? Did the company make custom-designed robots based on my features?

I looked again at the nude image. My tattoo of the word "PETE" was tiny but visible just above my left hip bone.

Impossible. Proof: I can tell you precise details of when Pete and I lost our virginity together. Exactly what it felt like. How it moved me.

— *Comes with a capacity for genuine human emotion*

I have a scar on my elbow from hurdles in track.

— *and physical response.*

I went to Andrew Sibbald Elementary School in Calgary. I played Mini Olympics with Jocelyn and Sandy in the playground on Lake Lucerne Drive.

— *6,500 gigabytes of artificial memory,*

I have a mathematics degree.

— *variable preprogrammed knowledge,*

I have family. Had a family.

— *Fiery plane crash.*

It was all part of my story.

I stood up, threw the papers and the card and the photos and the leather case across the room, and yanked open the top drawer of Pete's desk. Flung everything out. Grabbed his sharp silver letter opener and stabbed it into my thigh. I screamed as it punched through my jeans, through the skin, and into my right quadriceps. My teeth clenched together in genuine, throbbing agony. I pulled the dull, blood-covered blade slowly out of my flesh and raised it to my face to see the blood up close, to smell it. Lick it.

I stared at the tops of my hands. Blue blood vessels, as delicate as lace, were clearly visible through my pale skin. Those were not the electrical wires of a mechanized creature. On my palms, lines etched, both furrowed and feathered, that a charlatan might say foretold a long and happy life.

R9k4l. What did R9k4l mean? I'd easily committed the alphanumeric code to memory, but was unable to integrate it into my understanding.

Blood smeared the computer keys as I brought up Google and typed *R9k4l.* Nothing but random configurations and Twitter tags. Nothing. It's a lie, I thought. I am flesh and blood. I am breasts and toes and hair and lips. I hugged my knees into my chest, holding my warm, shaking body for reassurance. It must be one of those bad dreams.

Captcha

Pete would tell me about his dreams now and then, and I understood that they were stories in his head that emerged during his sleep, but I had never experienced such a phenomenon. It didn't matter. It's a well-documented fact that a significant portion of the population never dreams. And the rest of them could be lying, for all we know — making up stories just for entertainment and attention — as dreams cannot be verified.

I had to call Pete at the office. I needed to ask him. What is *R9k4l*? What is Cupid's Creation? Where did you get $250,000? Do you *really* dream? Who am I?

I picked up the phone but couldn't dial. What would I say? What does one do with this kind of information? *Bleep bleep bleep. Does not compute.* I couldn't wait until after work — besides, the guys were coming over for poker. *Hey fellas, here's another tray of wings. By the way, darling, am I a robot?*

Flashing on my computer home page was a banner ad for a new album release. Leonard Cohen. Is he still alive? I wondered.

That's it. I decided to use iTunes credits and download his latest album.

Leonard Cohen's a poet. He's old and ugly. His music is dreary, repetitive, predominantly three-quarter time. Yet he embodies a transcendent quality that only a thinking, feeling, fully emotional (and not always rational) human being could ever appreciate.

My heart would be touched by this man's music. What android is moved to tears by the sublime musings of this Canadian legend? I clicked on the Buy Now icon, input my name, address, and payment information, then scrolled to the bottom of the page where I was asked to read a series of random letters, squished together and mutated beyond recognition, and to retype them in a box to finalize the transaction. "Case sensitive," said the instructions.

Shit. A captcha. I had confronted these before. Completely Automated Public Turing test to tell Computers and Humans Apart. A challenge set by machines to weed out machines, captchas were originally designed by Dr. Alan Turing as a series of questions to determine if the communicator was a computer or a human being. The theory is that humans are capable of intuition and logical, experience-based assumptions that artificial intelligence is not.

A few years ago I had attempted to book airline tickets to Las Vegas for our anniversary, and I couldn't decipher the squiggly lines I was asked to retype.

"What's this supposed to mean?" I'd asked Pete, who usually took care of all the household online transactions. "It makes no sense."

"Oh, it's your eyes," he'd said. "Or maybe you have a bit of dyslexia." My vision is perfect, as are my literacy skills, and he knew it. But he edged me out of the way, completed the transaction, and we went to Vegas (where, come to think of it, luck was very much on our side.)

Wait. Case sensitive. *R9k4l.* Could that final digit be a lower-case "L"? I'd been typing the numeric digit one.

I shrunk the Leonard Cohen site, brought up Google again, and entered my serial number with the small letter "l". This time, first on the search was a page with the headline Cupid's Creations.

Please enter your password.

Automatically, I typed in "petelovesmargo."

He was so predictable.

Captcha

On the screen in front of me, there I was: R9k4l, (ID location: inner left cheek), registered as Margo Humphrey to Pete Humphrey, of 83 Spruce Lane, Kelowna, BC. Along with the same physical information as on my Certificate of Authenticity, and the same photos as in the billfold.

I limped to the bathroom, leaned across the sink to the mirror, and pulled my left cheek out as far as possible to expose the dark cave of my mouth. More light. A tiny mirror. A magnifying glass. Still, I couldn't see anything. I needed a brighter light. I used the telephoto lens on my phone, turned the flash on, and presto, I could make out a series of tiny raised ridges in the soft tissue opposite my back molars: *R9k4l*.

I could no longer deny that I was — am — a robot. A robot with a fucking sore leg.

In the bathroom mirror my eyes looked the same as always. Blue. Beautiful. Maybe a little more bloodshot than usual, but still mine, whatever *mine* meant.

Well, I thought, scanning my face, it does explain a lot. Like the dreaming thing. Like why I never get sick, why I'm not ticklish. Why I have no sense of intuition. No "street smarts," as my mother-in-law calls it.

"Hello in there!" I shouted at my reflection. "Who are you?" Squinted at myself. "C-3P0 with tits?"

I spent the morning inspecting my entire body in a full-length mirror, then with a hand-held mirror. I poked and prodded myself, looking for evidence that I'd been manufactured in a factory. Nothing, aside from my serial number. This company was beyond skilled. It took the discovery that I am not real to appreciate the workmanship involved in making me real. I wondered what the true potential of this body was.

By noon, I was hungry — yes, it appears my digestive system is organic and bio-equivalent. And despite my puzzled mental state, I felt compelled to keep my regular 2:30 appointment at FabuTan.

Lying naked in the tanning bed, tiny plastic goggles over my eyes and a fan cooling the air to a comfortable twenty-four degrees, I wondered: Should I thank Pete for bringing me into existence and treating me well for all these years, or did I hate him for lying to me? Did I owe him my allegiance? Or was he simply an ego-maniac and a loser who paid to have his dream girl built because no "real" woman would have him? Should I even let him know that I *know*? Would I age? Damn. I didn't even know if I was programmed to age! (Mental note: ask Pete if I will get old.) And if, as the brochure claimed, I consisted of ninety-four percent organic matter, what part of me was not real? Where was the six percent inorganic in me — spread throughout my body, or did I just have a robotic spleen or heart or brain that powered the rest of me? I knew my breasts were genuine — although Pete's brother has never believed it — I have the mammograms to confirm it. And why the hell did he make me a mathematician? Shit, I could have been an artist. A marine biologist. An astronaut. Only a dorky tax accountant would consider a mathematician sexy.

The fluorescent lights of the tanning bed snapped off and I pushed the lid open, feeling more alive than ever. The parameters had been pre-established, but I felt capable of exploring beyond them. I smoothed almond oil over my warm, tingling skin. I noticed the sparkle of tiny blonde hairs on my forearms and considered how *Homo sapiens* had evolved from the superfamily *Hominoidea*. Apes. It didn't mean people swung from trees and ate nits off each other's skin. Did origins matter at all? What about so-called test-tube babies? I didn't act or feel like a robot, regardless of how I came to be. They say that self-awareness is what separates humans from animals. And from machines. But what if you become aware that your true nature prohibits you from being aware? Does awareness negate programming? I tied my hair back into a ponytail, pulled up my G-string and hitched my bra. I thought about my co-workers at Kokanee and their fake implants. My mother-in-law and her pace-maker. Pete's poker friend's artificial hip.

He doesn't own me, I said to my reflection in the mirror on the back of the tanning-room door. *He may have commissioned me, paid for me and encoded me, but that son-of-a-bitch doesn't own me.*

By 5:30 that night, the house smelled of garlic chicken wings. The beer was chilling, the card table was set up, Sirius was on a classic rock station, and I was wearing the half shirt and cut-offs he likes me to wear when his poker friends come over.

"Hi, Mar!" Pete said as he burst in. As usual, I greeted him at the door with a long kiss. He removed his shoes and socks, grunted, loosened his yellow tie and, like every other day, he flopped down on the couch so I could rub his clammy feet while he complained about work.

"Oh my God. People," he moaned. "They are never satisfied. I do the best I can, and it's never good enough for them." Sticky little balls of black fuzz from his socks gathered between his toes. I'd never noticed the smell of his feet before, but that night my senses were heightened, and it nauseated me.

"So there I am, working through my lunch hour again, and Jim barges in and says, 'Humphrey! We need you to redo schedule 6-D on the Trundle claim. It doesn't add up.' And I'm like 'Add it up again, moron.' And on it goes. I swear, Margo, it's always something."

He paused, and I passed him his beer. "But that's boring. What about you, my beauty? How was your day?" I shifted on the couch and straightened my shirt. "Jesus! What happened to your leg?"

I had bandaged the wound, but blood was starting to seep through. "Oh, that." I reached down to cover it with my hands. "Nothing much. It was the vacuum. I tripped and bumped into it. Just clumsy."

"Let's see, babe. It looks serious!"

"No, really. It's nothing. I'm fine." I cupped the arches of his feet and took a deep breath. "So. I'm thinking of going out tonight, while you and the boys are playing poker. Everything's all set for you. And I won't be late. I mean, if it's okay."

"Going out? Where?"

I was prepared for him to be surprised. If not for my job and tanning sessions, I never went out. I had no friends. And because most of the beer events happened on weekends, he would always accompany me and park his car nearby to watch me work.

I told him there was a new book on epsilon – delta proofs that I wanted to check out from the library, and that I might just stay there and read it since he was having friends over. He tried to argue, but before he could get any words out, Andy and Jim and Pete's brother Jordan were at the door. They slapped him on the back and started joking about the hockey playoffs. So I simply waved, blew him a kiss, and left.

Captcha

With the windows of the Kokanee cruiser van down and Thomas Dolby's "She Blinded Me with Science" turned up loud, I beelined to Alley Catz, the bar I'd overheard the girls from work say was the biggest meat market in Kelowna. Happy hour was coming to an end, and my mission was just beginning. Choosing partners was easy. I went for variety. I went for new experiences. I went for that true human quality: connection and inspiration.

The first was a clean-cut young redhead with a tattoo of a tiger on his arm. Next was old and chubby, and smelled like the sea. Then, a tall, handsome Indian man, followed by a scruffy Australian fellow with a patch over his left eye. And finally, an Asian woman who was two-thirds my height.

It was 3:36 AM. and twelve degrees above zero with a thirty kilomtre per hour wind from the west when I pulled up to 83 Spruce Lane. A light shone from one window.

I walked upstairs not knowing quite what to expect, but not afraid. In fact, I was still buzzing from my escapades. All my senses were stimulated.

I found Pete sitting on the floor of his den, the contents of his desk drawer still strewn where I'd thrown them. My file was in his lap, his eyes were red, and his face was swollen.

"You're up late," I said to him.

"Margo," he sniffed and gritted his teeth, "you were going through my things."

"So?"

"You should not have done that."

I didn't respond.

"Do you have any idea how worried I've been? Where were you tonight? Who were you with?"

"Let's see." I started counting on my fingers. "First was Ron. Then Dirty James. Then Navdeep, I think it was. Then Antonio."

"My God!"

"Oh, and then Alex."

He let out an uncharacteristically high-pitched squeak, stood up and rushed towards me. I pushed him away.

"My sweet Margo. You've been raped. Sit down. Tell me. What did they do to you?"

"Pete, Pete, Pete. You're jumping to conclusions again. It was all my idea. I wanted to be with each and every one of them. In fact, I encouraged them. They were all interesting. And different."

He stepped back, pulled at his hair, and shouted, "You slut!"

"How dare you call me that," I hissed. "You *programmed* me to enjoy the attention of others."

"I programmed you to enjoy *me!*"

"So it's true."

Pete was silent for a moment. "Please tell me they all used protection."

"All this, and you're worried about *condoms?* I'm sure you programmed me to have STD immunity. And we both know I'm infertile."

"That's just it. You're not infertile. It would have affected your hormones if we'd — "

It didn't make sense. We hadn't used any form of birth control in almost four years of marriage. For healthy non-smokers at our ages, and with an average weekly intercourse of 4.5 times, the odds of not conceiving were less than 0.05 percent. "But then — why haven't we — "

"Because I had a vasectomy. It was part of the contract. For you to reproduce would be a copyright violation."

"What?"

"I know. It's hard for you to understand."

"Oh no, I understand perfectly, Pete. My uterus is trademarked."

He thought about it for a moment. "Yeah. I suppose you could say that."

"And what will happen if I do get pregnant? What if I want to have a baby?"

Pete took a deep breath.

"Not possible."

"Why not? If I have a biocompatible uterus and the hormones to support — "

"No. You must either abort before the fertilized egg has a chance to implant, or — "

Pete stopped, looked at me, and pinched a drip of snot off his nose.

"Or *what*?"

He bowed his head and whispered, "Or you expire."

I couldn't believe what he was telling me. "You programmed me to die if I'm unfaithful?"

"But it's okay. Don't worry. I have a bottle of morning-after pills. I got them when I got, uh, when we first met. Just in case this happened." He looked like a child afraid of having his favourite stuffed animal taken away. "Look. I can't lose you, Margo. I don't care what happened tonight. You are my life." He reached into his briefcase, unzipped an inner pocket, and retrieved a tiny vial. He shook out a pink pill. "I am so sorry you had to find out this way." He dropped the tablet into my hand and squeezed my fingers around it. "Darling. Let's pretend today never happened. Let's just go back to the way things were. Please?"

I went into the washroom and flushed the pill down the toilet. There was no need for me to swallow it. That night, Ron had read poetry to me. Dirty James took me for a motorcycle ride past apple orchards and sheep farms. Navdeep and I watched a sunset together and talked about heaven, then I danced with Antonio — Tony — on the beach under a cascade of shooting stars. And little Alex — well, she and I studied the complex fractal geometric patterns on a pine cone. Now *that* was really something.

Pete paced the floor of our bedroom, but I was exhausted. I curled up under the covers, told him I was logging out, and closed my eyes.

However, instead of simply shutting off like I usually do, the oddest thing happened. As I lay in bed, a series of images — my own private story per se — unfolded in my head. I don't know whether it came from within me or was delivered to my brain from somewhere beyond my physical body, but I was running late for an appointment at FabuTan. I couldn't find the car keys, then when I did I couldn't get the van started. When I finally arrived, I didn't have my wallet or my little goggles, and the receptionist didn't recognize me. "It's me," I said. "It's Margo! I have an appointment here." Then I was in the ocean, floating on a tiny wooden raft, with nothing around me but endless overcast grey sky and a flat grey sea. In the distance was a boat. I tried calling out to it but my voice made no sound, and every time I let go of the raft to wave my arms, I felt as if I would fall. As the vessel came closer, I saw Pete at the helm. He took my hand and helped me climb aboard. He gave me a beer stein full of fresh water with a slice of lemon and a plate of garlic chicken wings. The illogical story ended when I twitched myself awake. I am not sure how long I lay staring at the ceiling, trying to interpret the random cerebral events before I noticed Pete. He was sitting on the bed next to me. He'd gently pulled the covers off my leg and was cleaning the wound on my thigh. Then, ever so tenderly, he examined the puncture, coated it with Polysporin, placed a clean white cotton bandage over the area, and secured it with surgical tape. He looked old and worn out. Every line on his face was more pronounced, and his mouth turned down at a greater angle than before as he smoothed the edges of the bandage down and gently petted my leg over and over. I felt my own urge to reach and touch his arm.

"Thank you, Pete," I said. "I'll be okay."

Then I closed my eyes again to see what would happen in the next dream.

I'm working at H&R Block now. My cubicle is next to Pete's. I gave notice at Kokanee and started at the tax office the very next day. I love my new job. I'm the most efficient and accurate tax officer they've ever had, and I am assigned the most challenging cases. I get to wear comfortable shoes, a classy blue dress shirt, and a yellow scarf around my neck. I cropped my hair short, so I don't have to spend time styling it, and Pete says he loves the new, simple look. There's a heat lamp on my desk that I point directly at myself and adjust as I need to.

Since both of us are working, we hired a cleaner to do the mundane household tasks — the cooking, vacuuming, ironing etc. She's a lovely young girl. Not much personality, but she gets the chores done. I see my friend Alex, the woman I met at Alley Catz, on nights when Pete plays poker with the boys. She and I go for long walks along the lakeshore and discuss the infinite geometry of shells and the austere beauty of compound cubes.

Being in a marriage is all about compromise, trust, loyalty, and gratitude. I've given Pete my word that Jordan and Cara won't find out about the kind of investment he made with their quarter of a million dollars. And after our regular morning intimacy, I enjoy the pleasure of coming downstairs to a plate of eggs Benedict and freshly squeezed orange juice. He even puts the *New York Times* sudoku puzzle and a pencil on the table beside my plate.

My mother-in-law and I are going to see Leonard Cohen in concert next week. It took a few tries, but I even booked the tickets online myself. She says she's always wanted to see him, that she gets weak in the knees when she hears low, rumbling love songs. I don't know about weak in the knees, but I'm always curious to discover another soft spot in my hardware.

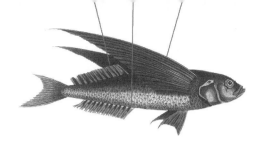

Dire Consequences

"EAT YOUR GREENS," SAID THE MOTHER. "You've had nothing but junk all day."

The girl frowned and pushed the vegetables around on her plate. They made creamy pathways in the cheese sauce.

"You are not leaving this table until they're gone, young lady."

The girl put down her fork and crossed her arms. "I will die if I eat this broccoli."

The boy sat, swinging his legs, smiling with his mouth shut, watching the match. He'd eaten his. And he liked it when his sister got in trouble.

"Quit being overdramatic. You won't die, honey. No one's ever died from eating broccoli."

"Oh, yeah?" The girl shut her eyes and ate the broccoli, piece by piece, lips pulled back so they touched neither food nor fork. Her face twisted in pain, and she dropped her ear to one shoulder as she chewed. She swallowed every piece, gagging slightly on the last one.

"See?" said the mother. "I told you. That wasn't so bad now, was it?"

The girl didn't answer. She wiped her mouth on her sleeve, went quietly to the couch, curled up under the afghan, and died.

From that day on, the boy knew he could get anything he wanted.

"If I have to do my homework, I'll die," he'd tell his mother, and she'd write a note to his teacher.

"I'll die if I can't have an ice cream cone," he'd say, and she'd get him a large Tiger-Tiger in a waffle cone.

"I will die right now if I can't ride in that fire truck," he'd say, and she would have a chat with the fire chief and next thing you know the boy would be sitting in the passenger seat, looking out from under a red plastic fireman's hat, grinning and waving at all his envious friends.

For a long time, the mother gave the boy everything he wanted. She wasn't willing to take any chances. Not after losing the girl.

But, as with mourning and passion, the novelty of the boy's threats eventually wore off, and the mother could not bear how spoiled he'd become.

"Hey Mum! Mum! I'll die unless I can have my birthday party in Disneyland," he said one day. "With all the kids in my class. Plus a few from soccer."

Enough was enough.

"Quit using that 'I will die' stuff with me," she said. "You will not die. You're just manipulating me."

Neither one of them knew if this was true or not, but deep down the boy was scared, so he gradually returned to his obedient ways, and she returned to not being such a pushover.

A few years later, the boy met a red-headed girl at art camp. Their birthdays were two days apart, and they had the same initials. They sat beside each other in fabric arts. They made papier mâché flying pigs together. They sketched each other looking like Japanese manga characters.

On the second-last day of art camp, behind the pottery barn and forty-five minutes past curfew, he told her she was the prettiest girl in the world, and she let him kiss her (mouth open, no tongue) and put his hand inside her shirt (on the outside of her training bra). They exchanged contact info and vowed to stay in touch. They swore they'd rendezvous before winter, even though they lived a three-hour bus ride apart.

"I feel like we can totally read each other's minds," said the boy. "It's like we have this connection."

"Oh my God, I know! It's like if I don't see you again, I'll die," said the girl.

The boy immediately raised his hand to her mouth and held it there, hard. Her head was pressed against the worn wooden slats of the pottery barn. "Don't you ever, ever, ever say that," he said. Her eyes were wide with terror, and her breath came in quick snorts through her nose. He felt the lumps of her braces through her upper lip. "Because you never know," he whispered, "and it's not worth the risk."

She tried to speak, but her voice felt like a warm vibration against his palm, and he could not understand what she was trying to say. When he finally let go, she ran back to her bunk and cried herself to sleep.

At breakfast and cleanup next morning, he was like a puppy dog, not willing to leave the red-headed girl's side. "I'm seeing you again, right? See? This is us seeing each other. So, you'll call me, right? Or should I call you first?"

"Freak," said the girl, then crumpled up the watercolour painting he'd given her and threw it into the lake.

The mother arrived just before noon to pick him up. Without saying goodbye to anyone, the boy threw his sleeping bag, backpack, art folder, a set of wind chimes, and a raku-fired ceramic vase into the hatchback. The vase broke into three pieces when his easel landed on top of it.

"Who cares," he said. "Let's just get out of here." Those were his last words for the entire drive.

When they got home, the mother made the boy a mug of hot chocolate and a grilled cheese sandwich. He slumped onto the table without touching either one. But he couldn't keep it inside for long, and eventually raised his head off his forearms and told his mother all about the redhead, minus a few of the physical details about the part behind the pottery barn.

"But I think I blew it."

"What do you mean?"

That's when he started crying, and the tears fell like rain. "I was over dramatic, Mum. And now she's gone. Forever."

"Hey, hey," said the mother. She scratched the boy's back over his T-shirt to cheer him up. "It's puppy love. But listen. You'll get over her. No one's ever died of a broken heart."

She gasped and covered her mouth.

The boy sat up straight, wiped his tears on his sleeve, went quietly to the couch, and curled up under the afghan.

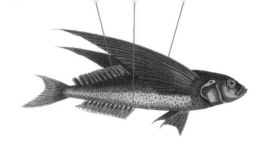

All-Inclusive

Joyce

The girl sat on the edge of the pool, feet dangling. Her collar-bones, her neck, the pale pink curves of her shoulders, sublime. Her hair was coal-black. Thick bangs framed her face, Bettie Page-style. Floyd would love her breasts. *Nice knockers*, he'd say later. I'd call him a tacky old goat, but I'd think the same thing.

The boy was muscular and lean. Something Chinese was tattooed on his arm. Wavy hair and a big smile. A ringer for Paul Newman. He wore an inappropriately sized pair of surfboarding shorts, but I suppose "a good fit" is no longer the fashion.

Floyd reached his bony, spotted hand between our deck chairs and gently squeezed my bloated, spotted hand. I didn't have to look at him to know he was thinking the same thing I was.

I smiled and nodded.

She jumped in the water. They were rambunctious, like a couple of puppies playing in fresh snow. Teasing, slapping, chasing, splashing each other. She twisted a finger around the string of beads on his neck, pulled him towards her, kissed him, then let him go and pushed him underwater, giggling.

He emerged with a gasp, and lifted her, squealing, onto his shoulders, his hands on her thighs, and proudly tossed her over backwards. Up she burst, eyes shut and mouth wide. Gently, he wrapped his arms around her and slowly untied her bikini strings at the back of her neck. Another squeal; more splashing. We weren't the only ones watching. Just plain delightful, they were. I wondered aloud if we'd ever had that much energy, ever been that carefree. Floyd said he'd like to think so.

Eventually they tired of horseplay and tilted their foreheads together, dripping, panting, hands on each other's shoulders, oblivious of everyone around them. Oblivious was a good trait. Otherwise things could get so bloody awkward.

Let's see, what would they be. Early twenties? When we were that age, polio hadn't taken Little Jimmy yet. The girls would have still been crawling around in the dirt. October? I'd be up to my elbows pickling, canning, tending the animals, putting the gardens to bed. Imagine, being twenty years old, flying off to an all-inclusive luxury resort in Mexico. We wouldn't have known what all-inclusive meant. Maybe some type of soup, or stew. Cancun would have been as far from my mind as diaper pins and war bonds would be from this little dolly's mind.

Sunglasses covered half my face. A sun hat shaded the rest. I didn't even have to pretend I wasn't watching. I took out my knitting and was free to observe and reminisce and prepare, while the needles clacked blissfully away.

Floyd was more conspicuous, as men usually are. "Patience," I whispered and he planted his moose eyes back into the James Patterson.

"Least you've got the book right-side up this time," I said.

He chuckled and glanced sideways at me. Even at eighty, my husband has a warm, beautiful smile. The lines give his face the look of a tightly pleated skirt, pressed just as it should be.

Our couple emerged from the pool. He flicked her with the tip of his towel. She grabbed it from him, giggling, tried to flick it back and nearly hit a preschooler running by. They covered their mouths in laughter and reached for each other, pawing, then collapsed into two deck chairs, angled to face the sun.

I gave Floyd his soda crackers, reminded him to wear his sun hat, and passed over the sunscreen. Really, it would be just like him to get sunstroke. Tonight, of all nights.

"Love you, dumpling," he said, pulling his hat down over his eyes and stroking my arm.

The proposal is always my part. Well, for that matter so is the selection — not that Floyd had ever vetoed my choice. I figure there's man's work and there's woman's work, and when you know your roles, there's much less room for conflict. I don't mind getting the ball rolling. I have my approach down pat. (It had only ever backfired once. Unfortunately, it was on the cruise ship, so we were stuck. It was almost a year before we tried again.) Besides, we both agree it can be just plain creepy coming from the man. There's no denying I have an aura of innocence. A stout old farm lady from the Ottawa Valley has her advantages.

Floyd fell asleep and I bided my time, watched them, and thought about what they would be like. How pleased Floyd would be. I sipped my lemon water and knitted. When our little mistress finally sashayed to the towel bar, I followed.

Jenna

I first noticed them over Finn's shoulder when we were in the water. They were totally staring at me and trying not to be obvious about it. Then again, so was that single dad by the diving board, and the bartender, and the three dudes on the pool steps. It's no big deal. I guess you could say I'm used to it. I never give it much thought.

The oldies basically sat there all afternoon, her knitting, him reading, dozing off, not even talking to each other much. Not that I saw. So that was kinda sad. I guess when you've been together that long you run out of things to say. She fussed around, put a hat on his head, brushed crumbs off his chin, that kind of thing. It took him like ten minutes to get out of his chair and go over to the pool bar for a couple of glasses of water, then she made him go back because he forgot a straw. He didn't care. He smiled at me and Finn both times he walked by. Sweet.

Anyways, she looked about seventy, maybe eighty. Not ninety, but who knows? Let's just say old. She was that plump kind whose skin doesn't sag as much as skinny old people because there's an underneath layer.

I was joking around with the towel guy when I heard her behind me, breathing heavily and grunting as she walked.

"Lovely afternoon," she wheezed.

"Sure is," I said.

"It's always better when you're leaving a snowstorm behind. I'm from the Ottawa area. You?"

"Calgary."

"I figured you were Canadian too. Guess our burnt pink skin gives us away."

She looked down at my stomach, my thighs.

"I know. I need to be better with the sunscreen. I hear it snowed in Winnipeg yesterday."

We both laughed about how we'd trade sunburn for snow shovelling any day.

"I'm Joyce," she said.

"Jenna. It's nice to meet you, Joyce." It felt odd calling someone that old by her first name. After Grandma died I didn't know anyone over sixty. My friends are all between nineteen and twenty-three. We're pretty much all the exact same.

We chatted for a while about the dolphins, the wild orchids, the ceramics, and knick-knacks in the market.

Then she lowered her voice, so I had to bend forward to hear her. "You are a lovely young woman," she said, taking my hand. "I mean that. I'd like to go somewhere to talk. Somewhere private." At first I thought she'd noticed I didn't have a plastic arm band, but for sure she wasn't security, so that wasn't it. Maybe she needed help with adjusting her hearing aid or putting on her circulation socks or something. Or she needed to log onto the Wi-Fi in the lobby and didn't know how. In any case, I wrapped a towel around my waist and we walked through the café into the Club Hilton. It was really high-end, fancy adobe-style, with terracotta tiles, stucco archways, and woven rugs hanging from the walls. We sat across from each other in soft leather chairs.

"Jenna," she said. "It's Jenna, right?" Her eyes were sunken, the whites yellow. "You and your gentleman friend appear to be very much in love."

"Sure," I said. "Yeah. He's awesome."

"And he seems to think you're pretty 'awesome' too."

I smiled.

"The two of you, you and — "

"Finn."

"Finn? That's his name? You two remind me of Floyd and me. That's my hubby. Floyd. A lifetime ago, we were very much like you. Except we were in the Lake of the Woods, Ontario, not a Cancun resort hotel pool."

"That's nice. Well, Joyce, it's been great to meet you, but I really should be — "

"What I'm saying, dear, is this: getting old is no picnic. The hubby and I are not as healthy as we once were. Life takes its toll, you know."

I nodded, let her talk.

"You see, dear, when you get to be our age, there are certain things, certain parts that just don't function like they used to."

"I guess it's good that you and your husband can still travel together. See the world a bit."

"The mind becomes a mite rusty. The memory department, oh, it'll play tricks on you. But the heart, well, that's where the hopes and desires and dreams reside. And that, my dear, is constant. Do you see? It's just as alive now, here," she patted her left chest, "as when I was your age. Young and busy and preoccupied with myself, with my own body, my own desires."

Why do I attract the crazies? Where was Finn when I needed him? I looked around, tried to think quickly of an excuse to leave, but she leaned close.

She lowered her voice, squinted her tiny eyes. "One thousand dollars," she whispered.

"I beg your pardon?"

"A thousand. That's what I can offer you and your gentleman friend, to permit us to be your voyeurs."

I accidentally swallowed my gum.

"Feel free to stand up and walk away right now if you are not interested, and I won't mention our conversation to anyone. All I ask is that you consider the offer."

"I'm sorry, Mrs, er, Joyce. I don't understand what you're getting at."

"You are a smart girl. I think you do understand. What I am proposing is simply that you allow my hubby and me to be present, but completely inconspicuous, in the room, while you and — is it Tim? Jim?"

"Finn."

"Finn, yes. While the two of you have relations. Nothing out of the ordinary. Your usual intimacy. I assume you are at the stage in your relationship where modesty and chastity are no longer considerations, but please, correct me if I am wrong."

"Oh, no. We're, I mean, it's not — "

"There would obviously be no contact between the two of us and the two of you. Nothing like that. It would be our delight to simply sit together and watch." She put one finger to her pursed lips. "And not to worry. We'll be quiet as church mice. You won't even know we're there."

I couldn't believe what I was hearing. My head was spinning. Was she for real? Should I bolt? Negotiate for more? Go get Finn? Call security? Say yes right away? Slap her?

"I've shocked you, dear. I'm sorry." Then she reached into her straw bag and pulled out an American hundred-dollar bill. "Here. I believe the Yankee dollar is universally accepted. I hope you don't mind." She folded it carefully it and pressed it into my hand. "Consider this a non-refundable deposit. Take yourselves out for supper tonight. Enjoy a nice meal. Have a bottle of wine. Talk it over. Padre Pescos down the street has wonderful seafood. If you decide to accept the offer, ours is cabana 12. We will be ready for you with the remaining cash at 8 PM. If you decide not to accept, enjoy your meal and enjoy your lives together."

Finn

Of course I called bullshit. There's no way. Have sex in front of that old lady and her husband? As if!

Jenna and I were walking back to Sunny Vista, the two-star hotel about three blocks from the beach where we were officially staying, along with hordes of American college students.

"Who do they think we are?" I said. "I hope you told the perv where to go."

She dropped my hand. "I thought you'd be into it."

"Have you lost your mind? If it was your sister who wanted in on the action, maybe." She punched me in the arm. "God. Kidding. But seriously, a couple of senior citizens? That's fucked up."

"I think we should at least talk about it," she said. "Who knows? It might be kinda fun!"

"Fun? Really? What about, like, morals? How is taking their money and having sex so they can get their kicks not prostitution?"

Then she called me a high and mighty hypocrite for being into it with my sister, but not with an innocent older couple.

"Innocent? They could be a couple of deranged serial sex killers. I bet she isn't from Ottawa at all. They're probably sex slave traders looking for naïve Canadian travellers. It happens! You never know, right?"

The elevator was broken so we hoofed up the stairs to our room on the fifth floor. The walls of Sunny Vista were thin, the cockroaches fat, and the mattress stained. It was an all-inclusive; the restaurant on the main floor was a Mexican greasy spoon. Two thin, scabby cats wailed for scraps at the front door. Our room had a shady balcony with a view directly over a dirty courtyard to another five-storey two-star and another shady balcony. Not exactly what we'd had in mind when we booked it, but it was a cheap junket and we each had just enough room on our Visa cards. I knew I'd be working double shifts at Sport Chek for weeks to pay it off when we got back.

So, yes, I'll admit, we needed the money. But there was something about having those two old fogeys my grand-parents' — shit, my great grandparents' — age, watch me screw my girlfriend that made me shrivel up like I was skinny-dipping in a mountain lake. Call it performance anxiety. Call it shyness. Christ, call it a normal, healthy reaction.

Jenna pulled off her bikini top as soon as we got into our room and squirted moisturizer into her hand. "You're taking it much too seriously. The lady was super nice."

I sat down on the bed. It felt like it was going to break. A gecko zipped across the wall beside me. "I don't care how nice she was. I am not going to let a couple of old farts get their thrills watching me — watching us — together."

"Look. I'm kind of flattered, and you should be too. They think we're hot." She sat on the dresser, crossed her legs, and smoothed cream onto her arms and shoulders. "If we're going to do it *anyways*, why not give them some pleasure? I think it's, like, our *responsibility* to share what we can offer."

"How do you know they aren't going to rob us blind while we're going at it? Or film us and post it on YouTube?"

"Rob us? Of what? Pretty much the only money we have is the hundred she just gave me. And besides, they're, like, ancient! Do you *really* think they're going to put it on the 'World Wide Web'? Puh-leese."

I guess she had a point. And I'm not a prude. Not at all. I've done my fair share of experimentation. I'm a normal, hot-blooded twenty-one-year-old guy, but there should be certain boundaries, shouldn't there?

Anyhow, I can't say I didn't enjoy dinner. We ended up at a funky little cantina and didn't even spend a quarter of the hundred. I must admit, it was the first decent meal I'd had all week.

It's difficult to say exactly when I started seeing it her way. By our second bucket of mini Coronas, I was thinking less of the harm in the proposal and more of the cash we'd walk away with. Five hundred bucks each! That would pretty much pay off the whole trip. Jenna needed the money too. It was me who'd convinced her to take this vacation, and this money might mean she wouldn't have to ask her dad to help her buy books next semester. Besides, what was the worst that could happen? I'd seen them both at the pool, and clearly I could overpower them if need be.

I finished my third fish taco and I realized I had no right to get all neo-conservative. This was something that my girlfriend was *into*. Why would I deny her this opportunity to indulge in a little exhibitionism if she really wanted it? Why would I turn down that kind of money?

By 7:30, she had me convinced.

By 8:00 we were standing outside the door of Club Hilton cabana 12.

Floyd, Much Later

To be honest, I don't get as much out of "show time" as she thinks I do. Like the bowling league we used to belong to back in the sixties. Now that *really* wasn't my cup of tea. But I went along with it for her, and she thought she was doing me a favour. In the end it got us out of the house and we made a few friends.

Don't get me wrong, I'm not complaining. Sometimes I think being in the audience is even better than being on stage: less pressure to perform. We've had some fine shows, me and the missus. I remember those two down in Mexico last fall at that Club Hilton. Or was it the year before? They were healthy, energetic. The boy, what's-his-name, her Paul Newman-type, he was nervous as a whore in church — or maybe I should say as a preacher in a brothel, ha ha! He had a bit of trouble keeping his Johnson in the game, but who am I to judge a man? Then there was the girl, young and black-haired. By George, she was hot to trot. A regular hoochie coochie dancer, with superb knockers, if I recall. It was a fine evening overall. Nothing like that pair we met in Maui. Poor girl got halfway undressed and changed her mind — out of the room faster than you can say Jack Robinson — her sad sack boyfriend standing there, buck naked and tongue-tied, shivering in the air conditioning.

But listen, this is the wife's indulgence. Joyce has given me a great deal over the years. Made plenty of sacrifices. Out on the farm, then in the suburbs, things weren't easy for her. I wasn't always the most attentive husband. This is her late-in-life hobby. She gets a kick out of planning the trip, choosing the couple, approaching the girl. She loves setting up the room for them, making things just so. There's always a rubber on the night table, flowers, maybe some champagne, lights down low. I remind her: not too low. With our bad eyes, what would be the point?

When it's all over, we thank them and Joyce gives them a little envelope and we say goodbye. Then, if we aren't too tired, we might enjoy a bit of hanky-panky ourselves. Not the rootin' tootin' swinging-from-the-chandelier type, mind you. We simply undress, climb under the covers, and do our best with what we have left. I suppose Joyce imagines me as this or that young man. If that makes my sagging belly and wrinkly underarms easier for her to bear, then it's fine by me.

Some folks use the Viagra. They say it can extend the pleasures. I don't know about that. Joyce says she doesn't trust it, says it's bad for my heart. Says she doesn't want me going and having another dang-blasted heart attack just for the sake of a hard-on. Says *this* way is more natural.

I suppose she's right, though it can be downright embarrassing. For example there was the time I fell asleep right in the middle of one of our "shows." I think we were in Cuba. Joyce had to pinch the inside of my arm to wake me up without the two youngsters noticing. Didn't want to interrupt them with my snoring, they were having so much fun.

They say a man my age can still *do it*, as long as he's not drinking too much and he watches his cholesterol. Well, I'm mostly sober and I don't eat bacon anymore, but I'm certainly not able to do it like *that*.

Here at home, we sometimes crawl into bed right in the middle of the afternoon. It's a nice place to be. Skin to skin. See if there's a spark to be kindled.

"Sports section?" she said to me last Saturday, when the spark wasn't there but the *Globe and Mail* was. "Thanks, dumpling," I said and traded her for the travel section. I gave her an extra pillow for her back, and one to rest her elbows on. I read about the Leafs' latest loss, some baseball player's trade, football scores.

Then her face lit up and she got that twinkle in her eye. She carefully folded the paper in half, lowered her voice, and put a hand on my forearm. "Take a look at this, dear. All-inclusive on special in the Dominican Republic next month. We've never been to the Dominican Republic, have we Floyd?"

Johnny Longsword's Third Option

THE MAN AT THE GATE TAPPED his pen on a clipboard in a rhythm that reminded Johnny Longsword of the opening bars of a certain AC/DC song off the *Highway to Hell* album. Or was it *Back in Black*? Didn't matter. What mattered was getting the fuck out. Getting back. That's all.

"We have an established protocol here, Mr. Longsword." The man spoke as if through a pinched nose. "It is the same for every living soul. Until we process your claim, check your credentials, and go through due process, I cannot authorize you to pass."

Johnny Longsword clenched his jaw and smoothed his eyebrows with his index fingers. It was bullshit. Normally he would simply slip the bouncer a fifty and be let through pretty much anywhere. Apparently the rules here were different. Besides, he didn't have his wallet. "You can't take it with you," Moira had once said. Turned out she was right.

He nearly bit it twice on his way back to Seating. His bare feet kept getting caught up in the stupid cotton gown they had made him put on at Threshold. Everyone was wearing one. Made it so you couldn't tell the men from the women. That's not true. You could tell. Just made it so you didn't really want to.

He dropped into the first empty chair he saw. The cushion let out a soft farting sigh. "Dickwad," he mumbled. The droopy-eyed grey-hair next to him turned, frowning. "Not you," said Johnny and tilted his head in the gatekeeper's direction. "Him. I'd like to know who died and put *that* tight-ass in charge."

"No use gettin' yer knickers in a tangle," said the oldie in an accent that sounded like it was from a black and white movie. "You'll get called eventually. A fellow gets used to it. Waitin', that is."

"Not me," said Johnny. "I've got shit to do. I've got a life." However, he'd left his phone at Threshold too, in one of about a billion lockers. He thought about his last Facebook post. He'd changed his status to *In a Relationship*, and eight people had *liked* it within an hour. Now what was he supposed to do: write *Stuck in an Alternate Reality LOL*? Or simply *Offline TFN*? He tucked his hands into his pits. Tried to remember how much food he'd left for the cats. Snowball and Mr. Tickles would tear open the bag if it came down to it. Toilet seat lid was open, so at least they could drink. They'd miss him, for sure. Good thing he'd left his Iron Maiden CD on repeat for them, but Pepsi would need her antibiotics soon.

The air in Seating was foggy but not humid, like there was a dry-ice machine on somewhere. It was hard to tell how big the space really was. He squinted to see better, but it didn't help. Seemed that damn gate was the only way in or out. How long had these people been here? Where had they all come from? Why wasn't anyone else freaking out? They were all pretty chill. Maybe they were baked. Maybe the fog was odourless weed and they were on some crazy trip. He inhaled hard.

"That's what I used to think," said the grey-hair. "That I had a full life. That people needed me. The wife, thirteen kids, crops to bring in: the whole lot of them counting on me, for everything. Then you get stuck here. There's nothing you can do." The man shook his head slowly.

Johnny Longsword shook his too.

It wasn't weed, he concluded. Otherwise he'd be hungry.

"Blessing is, least I'm not pissing pins and needles anymore," said the oldie. "Now that was a fiery place I'd never wish on nobody."

"Sorry?"

"I'm not denyin' it was me own fault. Lay with a nasty puzzle. Wench had the malady of France."

Johnny still didn't get it.

"Grandgore. The Black Lion. Don't tell me ye never heard of Cupid's disease? No matter. Even the pecker's in the maker's hands now. It's not so bad."

Which reminded Johnny, so he reached discreetly under his robe and felt around the base. Nothing. Bastards at Threshold had even taken his cockring. Was nothing sacred? "'Scuse me," he said to the man, then hiked the hem of his gown up to his knees and stomped back to Admin.

The gatekeeper was leaning over a filing cabinet.

"Hello? Knock knock?"

There was a bell on the counter. *Please ring for assistance.*

Johnny rang. He hated that bossy-bitch type who imposed their stupid little rules and morals on others. Moira had been like that at first. *Quit Hot Taboo and get a decent job. I don't care if everyone else does steroids, it's not healthy! Do all those cats of*

yours have rabies shots? Shower off that baby oil before you touch
me.

They'd met at a stagette Moira's sister-in-law hosted in her North Van home. She told him later she thought all strippers were idiots. "Shallow human beings. Male and female. I don't have time for shallow." She didn't care that some of his colleagues were putting themselves through law school dancing, while others supported sick parents with their earnings. It didn't matter that teaching guitar part-time at Twang and Bang Academy of Music paid crap and he needed the extra work to pay for cat food, vet bills, concert tickets.

"The human body is more than just a piece of meat you know," she'd said. "There's a soul in there too, somewhere. You never see a stripper peeling right down to the soul, do you? Makes you wonder if they even have one."

Moira had been the only one at the stagette who didn't watch the show. Didn't drink, didn't cheer or scream or paw or place a manicured hand over a glossy, gaping mouth, feigning frigid shock like the other women. Moira puttered in the open kitchen while he danced, her head bobbing to the music, and her bountiful booty rocking from side to side as she arranged prosciutto trays on the tiled island. He could tell that she was getting into the music even if she rolled her eyes at his fireman costume with the Velcro tear-off pants and the yellow hard hat, and completely missed the part where he dangled his blessed package the requisite six centimetres from the nose of the blushing bride-to-be, his hands clasped behind his head, abs like corrugated steel, his hairless twenty-minutes-three-times-a-week tanned torso the centre of everyone else's gaze.

He basked in the attention, yet it was Moira he wanted. A cold woman was his greatest weakness. Luckily, the sister-in-law was eager to assist. In the following days phone calls were made (Moira didn't answer), messages were left (she didn't return them), flowers were sent (daffodils, symbolizing good intentions), and cute jokes were emailed (who didn't like pictures of dogs that looked like their owners?). His persistence wore her down and, after nearly a month of courting, she agreed to have dinner with him (okay, it was lunch). Over hot 'n' sour soup, she told him that her name translated to the Greek goddess of Destiny. She may have just been making small talk, but he took it as a sign, and the next night they saw Antikriist at the Shaggy Mushroom Bar and Grill together. She said it was her favourite metal band. He knew at that very moment that it would be forever.

"Yes? May I help you?" the gatekeeper said, finally responding to the bell. He looked like a cleaned up version of Dusty Hill from ZZ Top.

"You certainly may. I know you guys run a tight ship and I respect that, but I'm pretty sure there's been a mistake. I don't think I'm really supposed to be here, and I'd like to talk to whoever's in charge."

The gatekeeper folded his hands together in "Here's-the-Church-Here's-the-Steeple" mode and shut his eyes dramatically. "Deepest apologies, but my boss is extremely busy. He has entrusted me with all aspects of front-end management." Then he unclasped his hands and spread them like he was inviting Johnny to hug him. "It you would like to file an appeal, I can process it and make a note of — "

Johnny started massaging his head. He expected a migraine. "Listen, Mr. — I'm sorry, I didn't catch your name?"

"I am the one they call Peter." He pulled his shoulders back. "Saint Peter."

Pompous prick thought Johnny. Then he recalled some story from the day he joined his friend Gordie at Our Lady of the Hills Sunday school. *This guy's going to be a tough nut.*

"Okay, St. Peter, Your Honour, I don't have time for appeals and paperwork," said Johnny. "I've got dependents."

"Ah, yes. Dependents. Loved ones. There's always something isn't there?" said St. Peter, tilting his head as if he had the same problem.

"Look, last thing I remember, I had just finished the Secretary Special — it's a noon buffet thing — and was bending down to pick up coins — loonies and toonies — from the stage. The bills they stuff into my you-know-what, but sometimes there's forty or fifty bucks in coins they just toss. Now I'll admit I'm not quite as limber as I was when I was in my thirties, but I'm healthier than the average guy. Anyhow, I get this stabbing pain in my armpit, right up into the pecs. Intense. I can't catch my breath. I grab the pole, centre stage. Go down on one knee, "Turbo Lover" still blaring, then nothing, and then this!" He waved his right arm towards Seating. "So obviously I'm not meant to be here. I feel fine!"

Johnny did a couple of jumping jacks to prove that he was fine. It was awkward, with his gown. "Wanna see some push-ups?"

"That won't be necessary."

"I can do one-armed?"

The gatekeeper blinked slowly.

"I know what you're thinking, and there's no way. I don't smoke. I work out religiously; I drink smoothies with whey powder. I even did some online yoga with my girlfriend." The gatekeeper kept staring. "I probably just needed a Tums."

"The appeal," said the gatekeeper, producing a multi-page form. "Pens are on the side desk." Johnny grabbed the papers. He wadded them into a ball which he tossed basketball-style into a wastepaper basket on the other side of the counter.

Saint Peter nodded. It *was* a nice shot.

Johnny put his elbows on the counter and leaned closer. "I think the problem might be my name. I go by Johnny Longsword, but that's kind of a pseudonym. On my birth certificate it's Lionel Littlehorn. If you check under Littlehorn, you'll probably find me. Then you can just reverse all this, I'll scooch through the gate, grab my stuff and the keys to the Firebird, and be on my way."

The saint bowed his head slightly, but his eyes stayed on Johnny. "We know exactly who you are, and why you are here. The list is perfect."

Johnny jutted his chin out, hands on hips, feet wide apart. "With all due respect, everyone makes mistakes. It's human nature, for Christ's sake!"

"Amen," said the gatekeeper with a surprising burst of enthusiasm. "However, regardless of our clients' personal ideologies, I stand by my boss. The data I receive is being continually modified. Your name does not currently appear in any form. You will have to wait here until Update. After Inventory." The gatekeeper went back to being poker-faced. "It's policy. I'm sure you understand."

Johnny Longsword's Third Option

Johnny stormed back through the immense lobby looking for a spare seat, fuckity-fucking through his teeth the whole way. He passed Games. A hunchbacked Asian woman with no teeth and a man with a short, black Mohawk and a naked woman tattoed on the back of his neck stood on either side of a foosball table. There was no ball, so they just spun the handles and watched the little plastic players flip around and around. A bony man with a buzz cut stomped his feet and shouted — German maybe? — at an old pinball machine whose flippers were too short to reach the silver ball and dislodge it from between two bells. A long-necked African woman danced to the non-stop rhythm of the pinball bells dinging, her eyes closed as if in a trance, her fingers twisting and jerking in a complex pattern of snaps, clips, and claps.

He thought of the way Moira danced the first time they went to the Axe together, arms over her head, fists clenched, shirt creeping up to reveal her pierced belly button. He thought about the way they'd laughed when she showed him her old high school yearbook later that night. He thought about the peck on the cheek she gave him at the door, and the way she told him not to be an eager beaver.

He'd been nervous when he introduced her to the cats. "I've gotta warn you, there are a few scratchers," he'd said. In fact, his couch was in ribbons. When they walked in, there was a cat on every surface. The back of the chair. The patch of sun on the floor. Three on the couch. One on the microwave. Two on the window ledge. One in the sink. Miss Muffet and Hubert wove staticky figure eights around her calves while Moira took it in.

"How many of them are there?" she finally said.

"Fourteen? Fifteen?" Sometimes new cats appeared. People who didn't want theirs would drop them off on his doorstep with a half-empty bag of kibble and a note: *Please take good care of Pepe. Thanks!*

Moira'd thought it was cute. She said looking after all those cats showed he'd make a good father someday. "Wanna get started?" he said. She ignored him and hoisted Hobo into the crook of her neck and made smoochy sounds while the tiny tabby purred like a new Harley. The cats seemed to balance out her disapproval of his job at the strip club. Then she teased him about how his clothes were always covered in fur — no wonder he always wanted to take them off.

They had plans together. He'd promised to meet Moira that night at Vinny's Vinyls to look for a Quiet Riot album neither of them owned. Then they were going to go back to his place, cook spaghetti, have some fun with catnip, and listen to "Cum on Feel the Noize" the old-fashioned way.

He had to get back. He couldn't just let go. He was just getting started. And the cats. Who would look after the cats? They needed him.

Johnny took a chair next to a black woman with blond hair like a scoop of ice cream on her head. He put his elbows on his knees, his forehead in his hands, and thought of Pepsi, lying there on top of the fridge, waiting, eye oozing.

"It gets easier," the woman whispered to him as he drummed his fingers on his head. "It really does."

A fat, caramel-coloured baby crawled along the aisle behind Johnny. He looked up at him with big baby-Gandhi eyes and started tugging his gown. "That is so goddamn sad," he said.

"Ah, the babies and toddlers never stay long," said the woman.

"But here? Kid should have a whole life ahead of it."

The woman hummed something that sounded like part of a hymn, then said, "Life is a sweet gift that comes and goes. Who knows what that child did with malice and intent? All sins, big or small, must be accounted for before our final destiny is determined and we are released. That takes time."

Johnny peeled the baby's tiny fingers from his gown, patted his dimpled bum, and the little thing motored right over top of Johnny's foot to someone else's chair.

He made a mental list of some of the sin categories he knew: Greed, Lust, Pride. There must be more.

"How long have you been waiting?" he asked.

"No idea. There's no way to track time here. With no sleeping, no eating, no bodily functions or demands, one doesn't get any older. But one does lose a sense of hours and days and years."

When one of your favourites needed antibiotics every six hours for an eye infection, you don't lose track, thought Johnny. When you're supposed to be meeting the woman you love at 4:30 PM at Vinny's Vinyl, you don't lose track of time.

"Why are *you* here? Are you some kind of criminal?"

"I'm a corporate lawyer."

Johnny snorted.

"I've had an illustrious career covering the sins of others. Justice here is weighed with a different scale. It's not like I committed a cardinal or mortal sin. Murder, for example. For that I'd've gone straight to Hell. I know that once my sin inventory is complete, I'll be cleared to enter Heaven. It's no picnic, the waiting, but it's better than forging steel weapons in that molten welding pit downstairs. At least here in Purgatory there's AC."

"So we *are* dead," Johnny whispered.

"Sure are," she laughed, slapping him on the knee. "We're all goners. In fact, we're more than goners. We already went! And this is where we ended up."

The woman had short teeth, ground to straight edges. Her crinkled skin was the same colour Moira liked her coffee. Her hand stayed on his leg; he could feel the heat from it.

"You look pretty alive to me," he said. It struck him that it came across like a pick-up line, one he was certain he'd never used before.

"That's because you're seeing things through your soul, not your eyes, dear. But make no mistake, you and me — all of us in here — we're as dead as they get. Dead as stones."

The woman told Johnny that her last day alive had been a sunny day in London. "Our daughter was dancing in the Royal Opera House in Covent Garden. We'd flown over for the performance. And what do I do? Look left when I should've looked right. Stupid tourist move. Didn't feel a thing. The fellow was driving a puny little Renault, but it hit me hard. Severed my spinal cord when I hit the curb. I broke more bones than they could count, and internal bleeding — well, you get the picture. Terrible thing for Raymond to witness. But you know what he did? He watched our girl dance that night without telling her about the accident. She was the Sugar Plum Fairy."

The woman sat smiling, her eyes closed.

Johnny Longsword was acutely aware of the murmur of voices around them. A bit of music coming from somewhere. Pages turning. Shuffling, sniffling, sighing. Some quiet conversation. A bit of crying, the odd burst of laughter. Now and then the gatekeeper would call a name over the PA system and someone would go to the gates, presumably to be let into Heaven. Or wherever.

But still, something in her story didn't add up.

"How do you know what your husband did after you died? Is there some kind of window from here? A portal? Or were you like a ghost for a while?" He couldn't believe the words that were coming from his mouth.

"Oh, heavens no. They don't allow spirit visits or even viewings from this department. Raymond told me about it himself."

Johnny looked around. "He's here too?"

"Was. Didn't stay long."

She leaned towards him so others couldn't hear. "Raymond's always had a temper. Well, it seems he tracked down Mr. Renault with a very sharp steak knife the next day. Got him under the ribs. Cut his own wrists later that night." She pulled her lips in, narrowed her eyes, and shook her head. "Foolish man."

"Jesus. That's terrible," said Johnny.

"Everyone's got a story."

They gazed silently at the menagerie of people — a few young, many old, most just sitting quietly, some wandering among the chairs, looking from face to face, perhaps hoping to find a familiar one.

"But your husband," he blurted, "shouldn't he have gone straight to hell — pardon the cliché?"

The woman tilted her head and gave him a mischievous grin. "True," she drawled. "He really should've, but I wasn't going to correct them. I got to be with dear Ray one last time."

It was exactly what Johnny needed. "Thank you," he said, placing his hands on the woman's cheeks and kissing her firmly.

As he did, he remembered: Moira, on stage with him at Hot Taboo, after he'd tried unsuccessfully to gather the coins off the sticky stage floor. After the hot poker stabbed his chest. He was lying on his back. He felt her hands on his head, and her face filled his frame of vision. Her frizzy blonde hair tickled his cheeks, and her eyes were slushy blue.

"You'll be okay," she was saying, her lips wet and shiny. She was stroking his cheek. Tears, or snot, dripped onto his face from hers. "I love you. I love you. I love you. Stay with me, Johnny." Then his eyes felt cold and everything went black.

She loved him. She needed him. And she'd been there. She'd been at the club. She had finally come to watch him strip, after all those months. He was both exhilarated and ashamed. He couldn't leave her. He hiked up his gown and returned to Admin.

"I apologize for being rude to you before," Johnny said. Over the years, he'd blackmailed countless people. He'd threatened, he'd lied and bribed. There was that thing with the MLA's wife, and the kindergarten teacher's retirement party that got out of control. But this was different. This was a real saint. He'd have to be respectful.

"For that, you are forgiven."

"You seem like a great guy, Saint Peter, and I know you're just doing your job, a job which I can see you take pride in. I'm sure it's a job you'd like to hold on to."

The gatekeeper lay the clipboard down. "It is indeed an honour and a privilege to keep the gate."

"I'm sure it is. And I bet the benefits are fantastic. Anyhow, I'll get to the point." Johnny lowered his voice. "I know there have been slip-ups. I know there've been people who've come in here who shouldn't have been allowed. Perhaps the name 'Raymond' jingles a little something? Hmmm? Or maybe murder-suicide isn't such a big deal anymore?"

The gatekeeper slowly reached a hand to his mouth.

"Seems that here in Purgatory either mistakes have been made or certain rules have been bent," said Johnny. Wham, bam, hot goddamn. He raised one eyebrow at the old saint. Let that sink in, buster.

Saint Peter started fidgeting with a three-hole punch on the desk, and cleared his throat a few times before speaking. "Actually, sir, after our rebrand, we now refer to the entire area, including Standing and Kneeling, as 'Club P'."

He seemed to be reciting promotional copy from a brochure, in a voice far louder than was necessary, and now with a British inflection.

"We have undergone extensive consultations with experts and redesigned the lobby to make it as comfortable as possible for clients waiting to enter the Kingdom of Heaven. We have the most recent lifestyle magazines, soft chairs of fine leather, musical rearrangements of popular songs, an endless supply of crossword puzzles I'm sure you'll be interested in. Oh, and sudoku. Did I mention sudoku?"

It felt good to have the saint by the short and curlies. "I'm not buying it, old man," murmured Johnny. "I'm not interested in puzzles." He did two-fingered air quotes on the word *interested*. "Not today. No siree Bob. I'm interested in finding out why a certain woman was at my club this afternoon." He was on autopilot, straight from the heart, no filters, no judgement or consideration. "In fact, I'm interested in going home and studying to become a veterinarian. I'm interested in asking the love of my life to marry me. I'm interested in getting tickets to next month's Gorguts concert. I'm interested in moving to an old farmhouse full of mice and sunny window ledges for my cats." Johnny paused, looked at his fingernails. "But, on the other hand, I suppose I could stay here and spread the word that rules are not always followed in 'Club P.' See if anyone else wants the rules bent in their favour."

St. Peter pressed his index finger against his temples and lifted his eyes skyward, moving his lips silently. Then he shook his head and pulled a key from an inner pocket. He reached under the counter and unlocked something.

"Well, well," he said, pulling out a worn folder and flipping through some papers inside. "Mr. Longsword, I just might have a solution to our predicament. It seems that, under the circumstances, you qualify for Option Three."

"Option Three? Now we're talking, Santo Pedro."

"Yes, there is a little-used third path we make available for those souls with more bravado than patience, shall we say. Of course, there is the risk of getting stuck in the Reincarnation Loop. However, under section 72-B of the Death Act, and with my personal approval, it appears you are eligible."

The gatekeeper gathered some papers, put an *Administration Desk Temporarily Closed* sign on the counter, and came around to the lobby side. "Follow me."

There were whispers and mutters in a variety of languages as the saint and the stripper walked through Seating. Johnny looked straight ahead. They passed the Club P Karaoke Corner, where the machine was stuck on the chorus of "Eye of the Tiger". They passed a shuffleboard game. Finally they came to the top of a spiral staircase that twisted down through the floor like an enormous DNA protein strand. Johnny peeked over the railing.

"Option Three?"

"It is a long way down. Some find they get too dizzy to continue. You may even feel the need to vomit. But if you can, keep descending until you reach the bottom. There, you will find yourself at the shore of a wide and muddy waterway called the river Styx. For a small fee, Charon, the boatman, will ferry you across. If destiny allows and you make it to the other side, you will have an opportunity to be reborn, possibly even into your own body if it's not too late. I must warn you, the waters are filled with tortured souls, and Charon offers no guarantee of safe passage. However, if you sign this waiver, release and indemnity form, you could avoid what might be a very, very long wait here and — "

"Good enough. 'Domo Arigato, Mr. Roboto'. Thank you for your service and hospitality." Johnny set the papers on a clear spot at the nearby craft table, where a Russian prince and a matty-haired cowboy were gluing macaroni on cardboard, so he could print his name and scribble his signature at the bottom of both pages, and initial the dozen boxes of small print that had been indicated with yellow highlighter.

"Okey dokey," said Saint Peter with the buoyancy and apprehension of a man who was about to have a thorn pulled from his foot. "Now I'll just witness and endorse these documents, and you are free to descend."

As Johnny turned to the staircase, he wondered how many others had been offered Option Three, and how many of them had decided it was worth the risk.

Then he stopped.

"Hang on. You said there was a fee? For the ferryman? I don't have any cash. I don't have my goddamn wallet. They took everything at Threshold!"

"Worry not," said Saint Peter solemnly, his hands together in prayer. "Someone on earth must have loved you dearly, Johnny Longsword, for a coin has been placed in each of your eye sockets. Two gold coins: traditional payment for the Ferryman."

Johnny frowned and lifted his fingers to his eyes, touched where his eyeballs should have been. Indeed, they were cold and flat like loonies. Son of a bitch was right.

He reached for the banister and took his first step down the staircase.

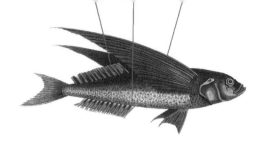

Lunch Date

THE GIRL AND HER MOTHER ARE at the usual table in the usual restaurant for their once a month lunch date. The girl orders a virgin rum and coke and the waiter laughs. The mother orders a gin and tonic. "Make mine slutty," she says and he laughs again, louder. The girl's face gets hot so she looks down and clicks her thumbnails together and does not look up again until the waiter finishes filling their water glasses and leaves.

The restaurant is dark even though it's the middle of a sunny spring day. There is a wall of mirrors with crooked gold marble lines. There are carnations in a small vase and an unlit candle on the table.

It's Thursday, so the other seventh graders will be doing track, but the girl brought a note and was dismissed thirty minutes early. This is good because she sucks at track.

"They want you to think it's happy hour," says the mother leaning on her elbows, her chin in her hands. "That's why they keep the lights down low. Plus it's more flattering." Some mothers have cleavage where their breasts squeeze together. This one's like an old chicken. She has a bony space between her breasts.

The mother turns to the mirror wall. Lifts her eyebrows. Twirls a strand of hair around her finger, puckers her lips. The girl could put her whole arm through those hoop earrings if she wanted to, they're that big.

"I only have one hour," says the mother. "Newburgs're putting in an offer on the Willow Creek condo. I've got to be there so Teresa doesn't fuck it up. Escargot?"

The girl doesn't answer. The mother always orders escargot and the daughter never eats them because she can't stand them. She tried them once and the chewiness almost made her puke. However, some things are not worth explaining every time.

"So. How's school?" asks the mother, sucking on an ice cube.

"Fine."

"How's Mrs. Monahan?"

"Mrs. Mulligan."

"Mulligan. Monahan. Whatever. How's your teacher?"

"Fine."

"How's skating?"

"Done."

"What? You quit? You quit figure skating?" She crunches the ice cube and swallows. "Ah, sweetie. You are so talented and you just waste it. You know if you'd carried on you could have gone to the Provincials? You could have been club champion? I know it's a big commitment but you can't just quit stuff because it's hard. Life is hard — it doesn't mean you drop out. Like I wish I'd carried on with gymnastics. I might be coaching now. I might have gone to the Olympics. But I quit. Thought I was too good for it. Didn't want to waste my time in the gym. You know what? There's a lotta money in coaching. Lotta money in endorsements. Shit like that. You just never know."

"But I didn't quit."

"Yeah, well sometimes people think they need time away from the things they are good at and all of a sudden they fall behind, lose the passion, and boom it's over."

"It's not over. I start up again in September. They always break for summer."

"Oh."

The waiter brings their drinks. "Here you are," he says to the mother. "And here you are," he says to the girl. The girl smiles a thank you. The mother orders the escargot.

"He's cute, eh? That waiter?" says the mother as he pushes through the swinging kitchen door. "Looks Italian."

The girl's nostrils get wide and so do her eyes. The mother winks. "Well, he is!"

They discuss the mother's new aerobics teacher and how she's too skinny and whether perms are as damaging as they say and whether clogs should be outlawed in this town and how the upper arms are the first to go. Some other people come into the restaurant. Business people, people on dates.

The waiter delivers the snails and a basket of nice bread. The mother tells him that his bartender pours like a girl and could he please make the next one a double.

"Ready to order your entrees?" he says. The girl asks for the poached salmon, but the mother says, "Two rib-eyes. Rare." The girl reminds the mother that she has not eaten red meat since November. "That's ridiculous," says the mother. "I'm the mother and you need your iron."

The mother closes her eyes, inhales, and waves the scent of escargot towards her face. "Divine," she says. The girl eats the bread. When the mother is finished, the girl dips pieces of bread into the holes of melted butter, twists them around, and wipes them up the side to get all the garlic.

The mother leans across the table. Close up, her skin is dotted like an orange peel.

"So. How's Phil?"

"Dad?"

"Yeah. How's he doing?"

"Fine."

"Fine?"

"Yeah. Good. Fine."

"So. Tell me. Is he still seeing that Tammy?"

"What?"

"Your dad. Is he still seeing her?"

"I guess," says the girl, smoothing her hands along the table-cloth in front of her.

The mother leans back and folds her arms and snorts.

"You *guess?*" she says. "It's not a *guessing* game. Either he is or he isn't. Either her makeup bag's beside the bathroom sink in the morning or it isn't. You know what? You have to learn to be observant about life around you. Otherwise life will just pass you by and you'll miss things."

The girl eats the rest of the crusts.

"How old are you anyhow?"

"Twelve."

"Twelve, eh. Shit. Hard to believe. Hard to believe." She rakes her hair from underneath with her fingernails. A few blonde strands fall onto the table. One lands in her gin and tonic. It hangs there, half in, half out. "Girls your age must be starting to get boyfriends, I suppose," says the mother. "Like Brooke. She's a little hottie. I bet Brooke has a boyfriend."

The girl isn't sure. She hasn't spoken to Brooke since sixth grade. The girl switches the forks around. Notices her upside down reflection in the spoon.

"Don't you worry about what Brooke's up to," says the mother. "You worry about what girls like Brooke are up to and you'll start doing things you'll regret. Mark my words."

She takes a drink and, sure enough, there is now a hair hanging from her lip.

"Okay," says the girl.

The steaks come. The mother saws off a big piece and puts it in her mouth. The hair goes in too.

"When I was fifteen — no, sixteen — I was the last one of my friends to lose it. The very last one. In the whole high school. Except for a few kids in band. But of my friends? The last one."

The girl cuts some fat off the edges of her meat. The knife is very sharp.

"So we're at this party, it was May Long I think — oh, hey!" she calls to the waiter, "how about a nice glass of Merlot with the steak. Thanks, hon — now, where was I? Right. The party. It was at Brent Tufford's house. His parents were away so that's where everyone was hanging out. And there was this guy. Jamie Olszewski. Coolest guy ever. One grade older than me. Beautiful jet-black hair, spiky on the top and long down to his shoulders. Like Corey Hart. And nice. Really nice guy. We'd made out a few times before but that's it. Oh my God, this is a good steak. Tender. Melts in your mouth."

She takes another large bite. Pulls the strand of hair away with a frown.

The girl arranges the steamed carrots around the mashed potatoes. The potatoes have turned red at the sides due to the blood. She can hear the mother's meat being chewed. It doesn't sound tender.

"Anywho, I decide enough is enough and I don't want to wait any longer. Besides, I knew he wanted me. Guys are so easy to read."

There is a dribble of juice from the meat at the corner of her mouth.

"So there we are, me and Jamie Olszewski, all hot and horny, but wouldn't you know it, the bedrooms are all taken and there's nowhere to go. So what do we do? We go into the upstairs bathroom and do it right there on the lino. Laid a green towel down. Bright overhead light. Hurt like a son of a bitch and then it was over. Just like that. By the time I sobered up I felt pretty proud of myself. Like I was finally an adult. Finally joined the club."

The girl is trying hard to think about what homework she has.

"Then later, when I met your dad, I kind of wished it could have been with him instead. Maybe in a nice motel or something. That's all I'm saying. Don't just give it up, girl. And don't do shit just because Brooke does. Trust me. Otherwise you'll regret it." She wipes her mouth with the napkin. "How's your steak?"

The girl asks to be dropped off at the side door of the school, says thank you for lunch, and watches the mother apply lipstick as she pulls away. There are still three minutes before the afternoon bell. The girl has French then Algebra. A boy is sitting on the floor in front of her locker, knees wide apart, Converse laces untied. He sees the girl coming down the hall. He hops up and tucks in his shirt.

Lunch Date

"I was waiting for you," he says. "Nice lunch date? How's your mum?"

The girl smiles at the boy. "Good," she says. The boy puts his arm over the girl's shoulder, and she puts her arm around his waist. She finds his back pocket, feels a race in her heart, and reaches her whole hand inside. She grabs a handful of flesh through his jeans and gives him a hard squeeze.

"Well then," he says and laughs so loud it makes people look as they walk down the hall.

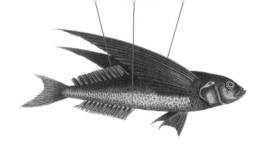

Lenny and the Polyamphibians

As usual at the end of the week, the accounting office closed at noon and Lenny was out the door by 12:05. He texted his wife from the parking lot:

Beautiful day. Meet me @ the spit?

Cant. Showing barker house. Wish me luck

U will b grt. C u ltr.

OK :)

The May sunshine felt too good to waste, so Lenny drove to the public beach anyhow, to the spot where he and Helen used to spend every weekend when they were first married. He found a smooth washed-up log, took off his tie, his shoes, and his socks, rolled his pants to mid-calf, rubbed his bare heels back and forth in the sand, and pulled a Thermos of iced coffee out of his bag.

He took a picture of a windsurfer hopping the waves in front of him and texted it to Helen.

Gotta love fridays!!!!

He pressed send and listened for the iPhone swish as the message travelled through the ether to his wife.

Something glittered and twitched on the sand at the edge of a shallow tide pool nearby. At first he thought it was a fish or a crab. He rolled his pants a bit higher and crept over the log. It looked like a doll with the tail of a fish. Or a fish with the body of a doll.

Lenny tucked his phone away and crouched down to get a better look. The lower half was definitely fish-like. Perhaps a salmon. He took off his sunglasses and held his breath. At the midsection, the thing changed from scales to — was it skin? And instead of fins, it had arms, with tiny hands, fingers like baby shrimp, clawing in agitation at the sand. Pointy shoulder blades, a long neck, and a tiny head with a tangled mass of blond hair entwined with sea grass. The thing lay face down, its spine curving and straightening with each raspy breath. Lenny glanced around the quiet beach. Besides the windsurfers, there were two mothers playing with toddlers in the shallows, an older man in a fedora throwing a stick for a lab, and a few people on towels, reading or snoozing. He gently reached down with one hand, gripped the scaly part of the creature, and flipped it over.

"Oh, my," said Lenny, yanking his hand away. The little creature had breasts. Honest to goodness titties. Small and sandy, but human. Volcano-shaped, like a thirteen-year-old girl's. And a face. Quivering blue-grey lips. She was pale, eyes rolling back, lids fluttering. Short, wheezing breaths forced her tiny ribs in and out like a premature baby's, while scales from the waist down sparkled in the sun.

"Goddamn, goddamn," whispered Lenny. A mermaid — dying right before his eyes.

"Stay there," Lenny said. He grabbed his Thermos and darted to the water's edge, dumping out the iced coffee as he ran. Soaking his pants to mid-thigh in the waves, he filled the container with seawater. Gingerly, as if she might disintegrate if he moved her too quickly, he picked her up. But before he plunged her into the insulated metal chamber, he held her in front of him, tilted his head, and gazed at her. The raspy breathing halted for a moment. She looked at him, bleated like wet sheep, blinked twice, and went limp.

Gripping her tail, he lowered her headfirst into the cold seawater. He could feel energy and vitality enter her body with each underwater breath, at first desperate and quick, then strong and steady. After pushing her the rest of the way in, he gently twisted on the lid, grateful he had brought his large Thermos instead of his Starbucks go-mug. The whole drive home, he held it wedged between his thighs — it was too big to fit in the cupholder in the centre console, and he didn't want to risk it rolling around on the floor or falling off the seat.

At a red light, he checked his phone.

FYI some of us have to work for a living

His wife had texted about the windsurfing photo.

U wont believe what I found @ beach!!!!

He hit send, and the light turned green.

Lenny darted into the bathroom in the empty main-floor suite and ran the tub — cold. He held the Thermos as if it was a lamp with a genie inside, even rubbing it a little. He was afraid to unscrew the lid too soon, in case the creature jumped out and flopped on the floor like a trout. Once the tub was full, he cautiously opened the container. Only the top of the mermaid's head was visible, surrounded by what looked like golden cornsilk. He poured the contents into the bath. He realized his mistake when the mermaid splashed against the porcelain and started twitching violently, as if she was having an epileptic seizure. He sprinted up to the kitchen, rifled through the pantry, grabbed a blue and white bag of salt, took the stairs back down two at a time, and poured the life-saving crystals into the tub until the delicate sea nymph stopped shaking.

All afternoon he knelt beside the tub, enamoured, watching the unbelievable thing, and thinking of names. Perhaps Shelley? Sandy? Aqua-Belle?

His phone buzzed:

Showing went well . . . thnx for asking — not! Going for a lane swim at Y.

A lane swim? Helen wasn't a swimmer. She could barely dog-paddle.

He didn't want to tell her over the phone. She would never believe him. He wanted her to see the little mermaid for herself.

Over the seven years they'd been married, Lenny and Helen had taken in orphaned kittens, were active at the Owl Rehabilitation Centre, and had "adopted" an iceberg to save the walruses off Greenland. On their fridge was a photo of Abdullah, their foster child from Pakistan. Most were Lenny's idea, and Helen had always been a good enough sport.

But on that first evening in the bathroom with the mermaid, Lenny felt himself fall into a kind of love and devotion he'd never felt before. She was a perfect, helpless, innocent creature, and he couldn't shake his eyes from her. He imagined a new father might feel a fraction of what he felt.

Oceana? Salina? Sea Biscuit?

He was hypnotized. He put his hand in the water and she swam circles around it. He didn't dare make a sudden move that might startle her. And when her tiny breasts, her slippery tail, or her soft hair brushed up against his fingers, he did not pull them back, as he did not want to make her self-conscious about her body.

Saltanna? Coral-Anne? Pearly?

He didn't know what time it was when Helen came home. He didn't hear the front door and was only vaguely aware of footsteps upstairs. He simply hung his arm over the edge of the tub into the water, switching to his left arm when he lost feeling in the right. Other than that he did not move. The spell wasn't broken until his phone buzzed.

R u here?

It was Helen. He wiped his hands dry and texted back.

Downstrs.

He heard cupboard doors open and shut. Some stomping. He should go up and say, Hi. Ask her about her day. But this beauty in the tub was truly a miracle. A miracle from the sea.

Miranda. That's it. Miranda.

U working out?

He was tempted to say yes. That he was using some of the exercise equipment she had bought for him. Just to make her happy. But he didn't feel like playing that game today.

No. In bathroom.

"Miranda. My sweet mermaid miracle, Miranda." He quietly spoke her name over and over. He held his breath when she popped her head up and smiled at him with her tiny rosebud-shaped lips, then he smiled back at her, and she tumbled under the water again. He rested his chin on the porcelain dreamily. His back and his neck ached from the way he was hunched, but it didn't matter.

The pounding of feet upstairs turned to loud clicking. High heels. Hard staccatos down the stairs. A knock on the bathroom door.

Lenny looked to the door and bit his lip. He couldn't show her Miranda. She was his. Helen would mock him. Helen wouldn't love her. He didn't want to explain the feelings he had for the mermaid. Why he couldn't leave her alone. Why he couldn't put her back in the sea, even though she really did seem perfectly fine now. He felt more alive than he'd ever felt in his life when he caressed her scaly backside.

Helen would bring up the foster dogs that had torn up the carpet and say it was only a matter of time before the bathroom pipes got clogged with mermaid shit. She would say they should call the Department of Fisheries and report the finding. She might even call him a pervert.

It was the first secret he'd ever kept from his wife. He'd looked into Miranda's wet, deep blue-green eyes and felt the push of a tidal wave that he could not swim against.

Lenny stepped out into the hall, closed the bathroom door behind him, and air-kissed Helen. "Hey! How was your day? How was the showing? You look nice. Why so dressed up?"

She raised an eyebrow. "Len. Slow down."

He smiled, wide, tight lipped. It didn't feel quite right but he couldn't remember how he usually smiled. "Sorry."

She sighed, shook her head, and smoothed her hair. "Whatever. Anyhow, it's Kirsten's birthday. Remember? We said we'd go out with them tonight."

He clapped his palm to his forehead. "Shit. Stupid me. Totally forgot."

"I figured. You better get ready. Now, what's my big surprise? What totally amazing discovery did you make at the beach?"

Lenny said something about an injured sand shark and how it needed to be in the dark in the tub and that it was no big deal, not as important as he'd first thought, and she probably wouldn't be interested because he knew she had a thing against sharks, but that if she didn't mind he thought he'd pass on tonight because he was pretty tired and Kirsten was more her friend anyhow and she should go enjoy her night without him.

"Suit yourself. But I hope that thing isn't going to stink up the whole suite."

"Oh, no. I'll keep the bathroom door closed."

"Fine. Have fun here with Jaws. Don't eat all the ice cream."

"I will. And I won't."

The front door slammed shut, and he was alone in the house with his mermaid again.

Lenny didn't go into work much the following week. The few times he did, he locked the door to the suite just in case Helen came home early. It was easy enough for him to arrange telecommuting, so by the following weekend, he'd set up his laptop in the exercise room/den between some unused weights and a rowing machine. He rarely needed to leave, and if he simply told Helen he was on the StairMaster, she stopped asking questions. By opening both doors, just so, he could hear the splashing from his desk. But most days he'd just roll the office chair into the bathroom, put his feet up on the toilet, and watch Miranda frolic.

Lenny and the Polyamphibians

Damn these shoes my feet r killing me, texted Helen one night from upstairs while he was downstairs with "the shark." *Foot massage?*

If I must, Lenny replied. He was being cheeky, but she didn't take it that way.

Fine then dont bother.

By the time he went upstairs, she was asleep.

Miranda was a busy, curious, playful thing — a constant source of amazement to Lenny. By the first week of June, she'd figured out how to turn the jets on and off. Her arms were getting longer, and her finger dexterity was improving. By mid-June, she could open the plastic container of fish flakes and shake them straight into her mouth. She'd learned how to balance the rubber ducky on her head, could swing like a monkey from the faucet, and if he was on the phone or at his computer, she'd fill her cheeks up with water and squirt it clear into the hall, just to get his attention, then hide under the toy pirate ship when he came in the room.

By July, Lenny knew his dear mermaid needed more to stimulate her emotional and intellectual development, and a bigger space to accommodate her ever-increasing size. So he moved the exercise bike into the workshop to make room for a Fluval 155-Gallon Elite-4000 Aquarium. He furnished Miranda's new home with antler ferns, a twisted root arch, three pieces of real scroll coral, one large piece of green bush coral, a mossy rock ledge, a sandstone cave, a tangled everglade root and a Great Wall of China underwater replica. Miranda swam from one attraction to another, delighted. Unfortunately, when the charge showed up on their bank statement, Helen had not been.

$1200 for fish accessories??? R u nuts???

Shit. It did seem like a lot of money. He knew she'd never understand. He should have paid cash.

Sorry honey. Accessories AND new tank. Plus filter.

Thats a mortgage payment. What r u thinking???

Tub too small. Cruel to keep a growing shark confined.

THE OCEAN IS A BIG PLACE FUCKWAD

That was the problem with texting. People reacted without thinking. He wasn't going to let her emotions bother him. She just needed to vent. She got funny when it came to finances. He appealed to her compassionate side.

Soon. When its healed. Dont be mad baby xo

Accessories?!?!? Jesus Lenny its from the spit! Give it some broken beer bottles, a few tires, and a shopping cart and it'll feel downright homesick.

Lenny turned his phone off, ran the tub again, carried Miranda, who was now about the size of a small house cat, gently from the new tank back into the bathroom, took off his clothes, added salt to the water and climbed in with her. In a loving — not a weird — way. She helped him feel calm, didn't ask questions. He could be silly and playful with her. She took his mind off Helen. She didn't think he was fat.

As summer progressed, Helen complained more and more about her feet; the pain had spread up her legs and into her hips. Being in water helped, she told Lenny, so she swam laps whenever she could. In fact, Lenny bought her a ten-time pass and a new bathing suit for her birthday. She used up the pass in nine days, then told him the bathing suit didn't fit. She wore ballet flats to work, telling him they were comfortable and still looked professional, but at home she padded around barefoot. Every evening she went to her friend Kirsten's house next door to sit in her hot tub. She said that eased the pain, but didn't do anything for the skin on her legs, which was greyish despite the Epsom salts she rubbed it with.

Lenny and Helen were still sleeping in the same bed, but as far apart on the king-sized mattress as possible. Most nights he didn't leave Miranda to go upstairs until he knew Helen would be asleep. But around the August long weekend, he did go to bed feeling frisky. When he reached under the covers, he was met with a kind of slime on Helen's hip. It wasn't a wet slime, but cool and slippery, like a pair of leather boots after you sprayed them with water repellent. He was incredibly turned on.

Miranda grew every day. By the end of August she came up to his belt. She was almost too big for anything but sleeping in the Fluval Elite-4000. But by then it seemed her amphibious nature was getting stronger; she was even beginning to favour air over water. In fact, the little scamp had taken to climbing over the glass wall (she used the everglade root as a ladder) and spinning around in Lenny's swivel chair. She'd stopped eating the fish flakes weeks ago, and had even begun to reject the sardines, oysters, and kelp. Although she wasn't too good with full sentences, her pronunciation of "spaghetti", "hamburger", and "chicken wings" was bang on.

As summer turned to fall, Helen and Lenny saw less and less of each other. She got herself a six-month unlimited pass and went to the Y after work every day, often grabbing a quick sushi combo for herself before coming home. Lenny spent evenings in the suite, and Helen went to bed early. He noticed six empty two-litre bottles of blue-green algae in the recycling. At least we aren't arguing anymore, he said to himself.

Lenny learned of Helen's hormonal issues when she accidentally texted him instead of Kirsten.

Still no period and fucking hot flash again. This is insane! Im only 33!!!! Too young for menopause.

Then: *Oops, wrong person. Disregard.*

U cant untext your husband. U ok?

She didn't reply.

That night in bed, he brought it up again. "Listen. About the period thing. Do you think you're pregnant?"

"No, dipshit," she said, still facing the wall. "I'm not pregnant."

"Then what is it? What's going on? Do you think you're eating too much of that salmon roe? Maybe that's affecting things, you know, in the female department."

She hoisted herself up on her elbows, misted her face with the saline spray she kept on the night table, then squinted at him. "I don't know if you've noticed, Lenny, but something is wrong with me. My vagina is drying up. And shrinking. My period stopped two months ago. My legs and feet hurt all the time. Sometimes I feel like my throat is closing. My skin is all weird. I'm losing weight, and I'm scared."

Lenny felt terrible. He hated seeing her suffer, but he knew exactly what was going on. He raised his hand to touch her cheek and couldn't help wondering if her eyes had always been that far apart or if it was just his imagination. It wasn't as if he didn't care that his wife was becoming aquatic. But what could he do? What could he say?

"Maybe you should see a gynaecologist."
She burst into tears and a bubble came out of her mouth.

Every day Lenny examined Miranda's body with the curiosity of a scientist and the intensity of a lover. He'd seen the changes that were taking place, and it would be denying the truth to say he wasn't delighted. Firstly, her breasts were growing, the nipples changing from pale, flat buttons to dark pegs, like sultana raisins on smooth mounds of vanilla ice cream. And there was her tail. The scales were taking on a skin-coloured hue, becoming softer, less slimy. He could caress her lower body in an upward motion as well as in a downward stroke, which he could not have done comfortably only two weeks before. But, most significantly, there was the twinning of her tail. It was as though two prongs, rather than one spine, extended down from her torso to the tip of her tail, which now ended in two hard bulbs rather than a single fin. Fleshy scales still covered the bones, but she was quickly gaining the ability to exert some lateral motion, wiggle-walk to the couch, prop herself up, and use the remote to find a show that interested her. A few times he had even caught her trying out some of the exercise equipment. The rowing machine was easy for her, but when she tried the treadmill, falling off the back, tripping as she tried to get back on, Lenny thought he might die laughing.

By Halloween, Helen's legs stopped working entirely and by Christmas they were completely fused together. Lenny rented a top-of-the-line wheelchair for her. Because of her shrinking size, he could get away with the junior model, about half the price of a regular adult version. She kept a blanket over her lap, and always made sure it hung down to the foot rest. She refused to let Lenny see under the blanket, but he could tell by the smell that her transformation was almost complete. Kirsten, bless her heart, had changed her hot tub to salt water (at Lenny's request), and the real estate office gave Helen an indefinite leave of absence from work. He rigged a CamelBak to the wheelchair, full of salt water. It wasn't for drinking, though. It was for breathing when his wife tired of air.

Because of Helen's increasing physical limitations and special needs, Lenny discreetly moved Miranda upstairs, and put Helen in the more handicap accessible suite.

"You gonna stuff me in your fancy aquarium with that stupid sand shark?" asked Helen, as the wheelchair bumped down the stairs. He had almost forgotten the story he'd told her months before. He just laughed and made up something about having put that thing back in the ocean where it belonged, and said he was sorry he hadn't told her earlier.

It was Kirsten who suggested that Helen have a personal health care aid.

So Lenny was finally able to introduce his wife to Miranda. The "nurse." That took care of two fish with one stone, so to speak.

Helen was bitchy about it at first.

Wow Lenny u r a piece of work. I lose the use of my legs and u get me Britney Spears.

But Miranda was kind and gentle with Helen, who soon warmed up to her. It wasn't long before the two of them started spending their afternoons listening to Enya, playing Go Fish, and watching surfing videos on YouTube.

None of this was easy for Lenny. You might think he'd be overjoyed to finally spoon Miranda every night in that king-size bed, his cranky half-trout of a wife relegated to the spare suite with the fitness supplies she had inflicted upon him. But he wasn't. Although he felt overjoyed to see the emergence of Miranda's nurturing, compassionate side, he couldn't look Helen in the eyes anymore. He could barely bring himself to answer her texts.

I thought I said sashimi. Tamago doesnt count. Thats fucking egg.

and

Theres something fishy going on around here. HA HA.

and

Im still a pretty good piece of tail right? Helllooooo????

Lenny and Miranda did all they could to make Helen comfortable, but by February she was acting deranged. Miranda defended her. "If your legs turned into a scaly tail and your ass became a dorsal fin, your first priority would not be maintaining civil manners and public decorum either." Once Lenny had come running downstairs to find Helen with the blanket over her head, spinning the wheelchair around in circles, crashing into the walls, and shouting *Where's Nemo? Where's Nemo?* in a high, raspy voice. Another time, Miranda had to use a pair of pliers and wire cutters to remove a rusty fish hook Helen had poked through her earlobe.

It was Kirsten who did the research that spring and sent Lenny the link to six aquariums with active acquisitions departments. *Do the right thing*, she wrote on the subject line. Emails were fired off to the appropriate people, and responses were swift. Although San Diego SeaWorld's bid was slightly higher than the Copenhagen aquarium's, Lenny and Miranda chose the latter because of the Hans Christian Andersen connection. They agreed that Helen would be more comfortable and respected in a place where the most-loved work of art is a mermaid sitting on a rock. Three days later, Arnved Thornsten was in Lenny's living room with two assistants, a cheque for 3.5 million dollars and a box of exquisite Danish chocolate-covered marshmallows.

"The vorld thanks you for this," said the red-faced, blond-haired curator. "Having a real live mermaid in our aquarium vill benefit both tourism in our country and the international marine science community. She vill be vell taken care of." Miranda and Lenny shook hands with Mr. Thornsten while the assistants wheeled Helen into a specially equipped marine handibus that had been borrowed for the day from the university's biology department. Through her tears, Miranda assured Lenny that Helen didn't really comprehend what was happening, and would be far better off in Denmark. He believed her, but was grateful nevertheless that his wife was no longer able to speak. Miranda and Lenny held hands as the handibus drove away. Kirsten watched from her living room window next door.

Miranda wanted to settle on a ranch in the dry Alberta foothills, far from the seaside, so Lenny invested in a post and beam home near Longview. There was enough space for them to open a small sanctuary that fostered wild animals that had been hit by cars.

Going hiking, texted Miranda from the solarium one day in early fall. *Wanna come?*

Sorry — checking on that poor grouse.

She put on her trail runners, her Oakleys, and a straw cowboy hat, and headed outside. The leaves of the aspens shivered in the wind, the pine trees slowly waved, and songbirds greeted her as she walked. Not far along, she sat on a log to watch some squirrels scamper among the mushrooms and juniper bushes. She took her shoes off to feel the squish of moss beneath her feet. As she stretched her legs out and fanned her toes, she was startled by a sound. A cry. No, a tiny *neigh*, like the whinny of a horse.

She looked around and saw movement coming from a pile of sticks and rocks. Again, the sound. Faint, but definitely equine. She took off her sunglasses, lifted the sticks, and cleared away rubble.

And there she saw it, lying on its side next to a piece of lichen.

The velvety legs of a miniature horse, with the torso and head of a man. She reached out her hand and tentatively flipped the thing towards her.

"Goddamn, goddamn," she said when she saw the full extent of it. The centaur slowly blinked at her with gorgeous, long-lashed brown eyes, then wobbled to its feet and started shaking off bits of dirt and moss and tree bark.

She took out her iPhone to text Lenny.

You'll never guess what I found in the woods!!!

But instead of pressing send, Miranda put down her phone and crouched lower, until she was eye level with the little creature. Its whole body was no bigger than the palm of her hand and its face was that of a grown man — a long nose, a reddish-brown beard and moustache, thick eyebrows. At the hips it became a stallion, with glistening earthenware-coloured hair and heavy hooves, pawing at the ground. It didn't speak, but reached its small, muscular arms out as if to embrace her.

"No," she said, and the thing pulled its head back sharply and lowered its arms. "You don't belong with me. You're a forest creature. Off you go." The centaur had no mane, but its tail was long and dark, and it twitched as she spoke. She placed one hand around it where a saddle would have been, and tenderly lifted it away from the rocks and sticks and placed it on the path that led to the clearing. "Now, get," she said, and with two fingers, she smacked the centaur on its rear haunches — not too hard, but hard enough to set it trotting off in the right direction.

She watched it canter away until it could no longer be seen, then noticed a text message had come in.

Grouse seems fine. Wait for me and I'll come hiking with you. Perfect day.

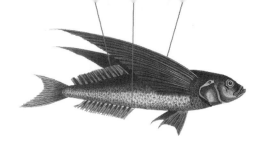

The Little Washer of Sorrows

YOU SIT IN THE WAITING ROOM, a thick bile-coloured envelope in your lap. Beside you is a chair that holds your wife's purse. Beside that is a chair that holds your wife. You didn't talk the whole way here. In the envelope are the documents they'll need: credit card statements, letters from collections agencies, mortgage papers, the lease from the car. You wrote *Greg and Shauna's Dirty Laundry* in Sharpie on the front, trying to lighten things up. Your wife didn't smile. There is a brochure rack on the table. The people on the covers of the brochures are smiling. Their lives are just fine. They don't get tricked out of their savings by co-workers they once called friends. Or invest in condos that were never built, or have boat repair bills up to here. Or, admit it, play poker online late at night when you should have been marking papers.

You reach over the purse and gently place your hand on your wife's forearm. You want to tell her that this is a good thing, that it will all work out, that the harassing phone calls and threatening letters will finally stop. And, in seven years, it will be wiped from your credit ratings.

But you've said that a thousand times. What you really want is for her to say those things to you. Anyhow, she pulls her hand away and crosses her arms.

The waiting room feels like a morgue. There's a stale smell of death and perfume in the air. You shut your eyes and wrinkle your nose. Perhaps this is how it all ends. Perhaps it's already done, and you're just tying up the loose ends. Perhaps you're here to identify your own body. If so, you would tuck a four-leaved clover into the casket. For better luck in the next life. Can't hurt, can it?

A woman comes around the corner and interrupts your funereal thoughts. It takes a moment to register who she really is. You can barely breathe. She holds your gaze and, finally, speaks.

"You must be the Houldens," she says. "Greg and Shauna?"

You nod, mouth a gaping hole. *And you must be the Little Washer of Sorrows.* But you don't say it. You don't dare say a word. Here, in the chrome and glass and maroon MNP office stands perhaps the most dreaded and best known of the Irish faeries. Although her badge says Assistant Estate Manager, and her voice is squeakier than you would have imagined, she is an ancient spirit. The banshee. You know the legend well. In fact, you taught an Irish Folklore class at the community college not long ago. A banshee spends her life at the shores of a river, washing clothes of the soon-to-die, constantly wailing her sorrowful cry.

Your wife stands to greet this mournful spirit. "How are you?" she says, as if to a friend at Curves. The backs of your legs are magnetized to the chair; it takes great effort to stand up. Your wife looks your way and does that tilting thing with her head that means: *you are a graceless idiot.*

86

"Fine thanks," says the Little Washer of Sorrows. "I'm Fiona." She's wearing a shamrock-green blouse, ruffles framing her ample cleavage, and a shiny grey jacket. The whites of her eyes are pinkish, no doubt from continuously weeping as she washes the garments of men who are doomed to perish. Banshees are said to be one of the few faerie spirits to marry mortals. You notice that there is a ring on her finger. There is no saliva in your mouth.

"Fiona O'Sullivan. It's good to finally meet you, after all those emails," she says, reaching her hand towards you now. "I'm glad you could come in today. I'll be guiding you through the entire process."

O'Sullivan, indeed. Not certain if it's safe to touch flesh to flesh, you say something about having a cold and that you'd better not shake her hand because you would hate for her to catch something from you. Your wife turns and does that thing with one eyebrow that means: *Yeah? Since when?*

The banshee leads you to the conference room, waves one arm over the chairs you are to sit in as if casting a spell, and offers you each a coffee. You stare at her. "Hag of the Dribble" is another translation of her name (Welsh), but this spirit's long, wavy red hair and pale complexion indicate that she is from much farther north. This spirit is no hag.

You place the eight-by-ten packet of your life's misery and failures on the table, face down. Conundrum: should you give her an indication that you recognize her? That you know who she truly is? Would this endanger you? She might be impressed at both your knowledge of Gaelic lore and your powers of intuition, but obviously she must keep her true identity hidden in this professional incarnation. You decide it best not to let the cat out of the bag. You have no idea whether she has a message of mortality for you, or whether this is simply what an Irish legend must do to survive in twenty-first century Vancouver — take a job as an Assistant Estate Manager at an insolvency firm.

Whichever is it, you are simultaneously awestruck and terrified.

There is talk between this woman and your now chatty wife of traffic and weather and her kids' ages compared to your kids' ages. There are questions about cream and sugar in coffee. She has no accent, but there's an odd lilt to her speech. Like she is covering up an accent. Pretending to be Canadian. She's good, this Fiona. Just how good? you wonder. You decide to test her a little.

"So, what's the craic then? Are we just barrellin' round, now that it's all gone arseways, or can we make a right go of it?"

Fiona and your wife both stare at you.

"Hello?" says your wife.

"Um, I beg your pardon?" says the other.

You cough. "It's just . . . I mean, we're going to get through this, right? People survive bankruptcy, don't they?"

"Absolutely," says the Little Washer, without making eye contact. "But before we get to your personal file, I'd just like to review the Bankruptcy Law in Canada with you. And please, stop me anytime. From what you've told me in your emails, your case seems fairly straightforward, but I want to make sure it's all clear, so I'll just read you a bit of this."

You remind yourself of the common misconception that banshees *cause* death. In truth, they only wail when death is already imminent. The wailing and occasional rapping of garments on the windowpane of the about-to-die is a warning.

A prophesy, not a threat. You use this to try to reassure yourself, however the nauseous feeling does not subside. You grip your thighs and breathe through your mouth. It does not help.

"One of the main purposes of bankruptcy law in Canada is to give a person a fresh financial start. This is good for the debtor and his family and also good for society."

Sitting across from her, you can't see whether this woman has one nostril or two. That would confirm it. You try to slide lower in your chair to get a better angle, but she's holding her head in a way that makes it hard to tell.

"It's really a win-win situation. If there were not the opportunity for a fresh financial start then the debtor might be forced into the underground economy, with a consequent loss of taxes paid to the government and the lost opportunity for the debtor to build wealth, such as owning a home."

Your wife's chin starts to quiver. She sniffles and apologizes to the Little Washer of Sorrows. Says she can't help it. That it's been so tough. "Will we lose our home? What about the RESP? I can't believe this is happening. I mean, we both have good jobs. We both work so hard. A few bad decisions, a flat real estate market, and now this? It just isn't fair!"

Her timing is perfect. You lean across the table to reach for a Kleenex, and by angling your head to the left, you are afforded the opportunity to get a look under the Little Washer of Sorrows' nose. Two nostrils. *Hmmm. Weird.* But that doesn't change anything. It is also said that they may have a single large tooth. Well, this creature definitely has a full set, normal sized. You pass a tissue to your wife, and she blows her nose then dabs her eyes.

Besides, not all banshees are the same. This one obviously does her keening wail of woe on a part-time basis.

"Shauna. Hey. It's okay," she says, as your wife crumples the Kleenex in her fist, takes a shaky breath and looks down. "There's no need to feel ashamed. Look. I know it's hard. But it is also important to realize that you are not alone in your financial challenges." She glances at her clipboard again. "Over the past twenty years, we've helped thousands of individuals in BC by providing debt relief and helping them achieve a fresh financial start."

She stands up, walks to the window that looks into the reception area, and closes the blinds. "Here. Let's have a little privacy." Your wife looks at you sadly. You look at the banshee's feet. She has webbed toes, of course, but is wearing closed toe pumps so you can't see them. You look at her ankles anyhow. Delicate. Her calves, strong and round. Nothing like you'd imagine a prophet of doom's legs to be.

You should ask to be assigned a different estate manager. Right now. You should tell your wife that you need to go to a different company. You should tell her to just trust you. You should make something up. But you feel an erection coming on and can't make a decision. You look at the ceiling and think of golf so it will go away.

There is talk about it all being quite simple. Something about bankruptcy fees set by the government, mandatory earnings and expenditure reports, and a maximum monthly income. Your wife sees you squirm and sees your red face and knows you too well. She kicks you under the table, which means: *you are a pig.*

"Now, if you'll excuse me," says the Little Washer of Sorrows, "I'm going to get a few things for you to sign, and make a copy of your paperwork. And, by the way, I've got to warn you, our photocopier is rather loud. It really needs to be repaired."

She picks up the envelope and flips it to the side on which you wrote *Greg and Shauna's Dirty Laundry*. "Hilarious," she says. "Now, let's see if we can get those stains out." She closes the door gently behind her.

Moments later, a heart-stopping cry emanates from the reception area. The wail of doom. The cry of the banshee. The prophesy of the Little Washer of Sorrows, about to unfold. You drop from your chair like a man shot, throw your arms around your wife's legs, and bury your face in her thighs. She pulls back, unaware that this is the end. You look up at her, your face contorted with dread. Her body is rigid, her hands in stick-'em-up position. She frowns and it means: *what the hell is wrong with you?* She doesn't understand.

"I love you, Shauna," you bawl into her skirt. "I'm so sorry. Please forgive me, my love. I've ruined everything. I want more time. I want to make it up to you. You deserve better. Please, find someone better."

She could push you away; insist you die lonely and unloved. She could blame you or scream or lash out. Or simply ignore you.

But she doesn't.

She softens and gently leans into you. She puts one hand on your back, the other on your head. Then she too comes off her chair and you are both kneeling on the floor, embracing under the fluorescent lights that feel like the final setting sun.

"Greg. Hey. Honey. It's okay. We're going to be okay. We're in this together. I'm still here. We'll get through this. It's going to be fine. Shhhhh." The lamentation from beyond continues. It is a moan, a grind, a scream, all in one. It sounds like the keening of Uilleann pipes at an Irish wake. Your wake. Your near-widow is weeping too. She squeezes her arms around your body and there is a flood in your heart, which might be the heart attack, might be the stroke. Your eyes sting and your throat is clamped shut and you can't remember the last time you've really held each other. You could stay in this very embrace for all eternity.

Suddenly, the wailing stops.

You lift your head from Shauna's neck and tentatively glance from side to side. Through your tears you see everything is as it was. The conference table. The chairs. The lights. Everything except this woman in your arms. You look into her sparkling green eyes. So beautiful. So perfect. You are still alive, yet being held by an angel. An angel who is your wife.

Fiona O'Sullivan opens the door. "Oh, jeez! Sorry to interrupt."

"It's okay," you whisper, not looking her way. "It's all okay."

"Stupid copier's jammed. I'll be another minute. I want to make sure there are multiple copies of everything."

When the wailing of the banshee starts up again, you settle your hand upon your heart. You have been wrong before.

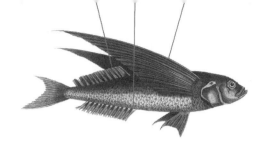

Candy on the Jesus Bar

A TALL MAN IN A TUX and cowboy boots, shiny black hair, and mirrored sunglasses leaned against the side of a long trailer, sucking on a cigarette. One knee bent, like a number four, he looked just like the guy on that billboard.

I tucked a stray chunk of hair behind my ear, checked my fly and wiped my nose on my sleeve before he saw me.

Back there, behind the scenes, it smelled like mini donuts, cigarettes, sweat, and puke. This was the brain of the midway, extension cords twisted across the stained asphalt like nerves in a bio textbook diagram. You could still hear muffled sirens from the Tilt-A-Whirl, screaming from the Forbidden Palace of Horrors, the blare of carnies asking "pretty ladies" and "big fellas" to step-right-up and try their luck.

The man slid his glasses down his nose. His eyes were Gatorade blue.

"Excuse me. Hi. Hello." I bit my lip. "Is this 6N? They told me to come to 6N."

He looked at my runners, then to the rest of me. I had to pee. "You Katherine?" said the man. I didn't know what to do with my hands.

"Yeah. Yes. That's me. Are you Reggie? The Hire-A-Student man said you were looking for someone to help with promotions? I hope its okay; I didn't bring a resume or anything." I was talking too much. Too fast. I'd never had a job interview before.

"Come closer. I won't bite." He took off his sunglasses and crushed the cigarette under the heel of his boot. He had a moustache that went past the sides of his mouth. Bells rang out and Hall and Oates' "Maneater" blasted across the midway.

"Let your hair down, Katherine."

I yanked the elastic out and wrapped it around my wrist. My hair fell frizzy across my shoulders. If he liked me, this would be my first real job, not counting babysitting for the Grievers, selling egg cartons of golf balls we found in the river, or painting Judy's parents' fence. Hire-A-Student said they'd pay me $3.75 per hour, and that I'd be finished by 9 PM, what with being a minor. That was fine; Dad said he'd meet me at the main gate at 9:20. Hire-A-Student said I'd get a cheque at the end of Stampede Week, minus taxes and whatever.

Reggie folded his arms and inhaled with a whistle. He reminded me of one of those guys who hangs out in the junior high parking lot, who the principal has to ask to leave so he doesn't bother people. A bit pervy, maybe, and older, but all right. Probably drove a nice Camaro too.

"Take off your shirt."

I put my backpack down and pulled my hoodie over my head. It was promo work, so I'd probably get a uniform. What if I saw Judy and Laura? Doing *promo work*. Judy had a job cleaning her dad's office on Saturdays, which didn't really count because it was her dad. I'd had to give my social insurance number. SIN, they called it.

I straightened out my T-shirt with a tug.

"Nice," Reggie said, nodding. "C'mere. Into my office."

That was it? Didn't seem like much of a job interview, but Dad always said they'd take anyone with a pulse at the Calgary Stampede.

The trailer, and the one beside it and the one beside that, was dusty and plain. Just big moving trucks, really. Not what you'd expect from the fancy stuff on the other side — the side people saw. Like a big secret that you're totally dying to find out, but when they finally tell you, it's something you already knew, or you didn't even care about in the first place.

I followed him up some clangy steps and through a metal door.

What a mess. Sagging shelves piled with boxes. Half-sized lockers, some with bent doors hanging open. A mini-fridge with an old corn dog on top. A card table covered with magazines. There was a fire extinguisher on the floor and a grey towel hanging on the back of the bathroom door.

I really had to pee, but didn't want to make a bad impression.

"Been through the rest of the midway yet?" asked Reggie tossing his keys onto a *Tiger Beat* on the table.

"No. Not really. A bit, I guess. They didn't tell me what kind of ride I'd be working at."

"Well, we're not a ride," said Reggie, folding a stick of gum into his mouth slowly and looking down at me. He was so close I could see that his eyes were pretty bloodshot. I backed up, but the room was too small to go far.

"We're an experience, Katherine. We're a ride for the mind and the heart." He spoke like I didn't understand English. "We don't take your money just to toss you around and make you sick or scare the shit outta you. No ma'am. This is where you come and expand your whole world. Open up your universe. At the Human Oddities Show, we rock your soul. We like to shake up your notion of what's normal. What's acceptable. We show people that not everyone in this civilized society fits into their little cookie cutters. We're not all Barbie and Ken. Used to be called the Great North American Freak Show, before political correctness sucked the spirit from the world and turned us all into vanilla-pudding-eating lemmings."

He snapped his gum.

"Okay." It was all I could think of.

He motioned for me to follow him out of the back office into the main section of the trailer. Burgundy velvet drapes hung from the ceiling to the floor on both sides, making a long hallway between them. It looked elegant, dark, and warm, but smelled like the boys' locker room.

"The Attractions are just finishing their break. Customers'll be coming through soon," said Reggie. "Trish'll get you ready. I need you out front in ten."

He pulled apart a section of curtain on our left. I gasped, then tried not to. The most enormous person I had ever seen sat in a huge wooden chair, surrounded by cushions. Only a blue rope fence like the kind in movie lineups separated me from him.

"Tiny Tim: Fattest Man on Earth! 960 Pounds and Still Growing!" read the sign. He wore canvas pants that didn't go past his knees, which were as big as beach balls. Folds of pink flesh fell over themselves. He looked like he was made of wax and melting. There were three unopened pizza boxes, a couple of subs wrapped up, and a pitcher of something pink on a table next to him. He was looking seriously at his fingernails.

"Hey, buddy. Where's Trish?" said Reggie.

"Dunno," said the fattest man on earth. "Haven't seen her."

"He's good people," whispered Reggie, pulling the curtain shut. "Star attraction. Everybody loves watching him eat."

I stood back as he pulled another section of curtain aside. A sign said "Boneless Betty," but there was no one there — just a folding chair on a black mat, a couple of hula hoops, a ladder, and a plastic box the size of a footstool.

In the next room, a woman dressed like a belly dancer in silk tassels and tiny bells was gargling, shaking her hair back. A display of swords and knives and a jar of Vaseline lay on a table beside her. One sword had a blade as long as my arm.

"Gigi. Where's Trish?" The woman shrugged her shoulders, still gargling. She didn't look at us.

"Probably in with Fireproof Al," said Reggie.

A puffy blonde woman in a red gown burst through a curtain-room near the other end of the trailer, yelling over her shoulder "Get your own goddamn gloves, Al. Quit whining! I swear, you are such a girl sometimes." She saw us, put her hands on her hips, and smiled at me, arms outstretched. "And who is this little peach?"

"New promo girl," said Reggie. "Get her prepped. I'll deal with Mr. Asbestos."

"Thanks, Reg. C'mon, dear. I'm Trish."

Back in the office, she rifled through a box. "Costume's in here somewhere. Now, what size are your feet?"

"Seven, I think. Or seven and a half."

"Perfect. Here we go. Put your stuff in a locker and come get me when you're done. There's the bathroom. Use it. I'll be in with Tim."

"Tim?"

"The fat guy."

I gently parted the curtain to Tim's room. Trish was standing on his chair, leaning over him, wiping under the folds of his chin with a towelette. His eyes were like raisins in a bun.

I cleared my throat to get her attention.

"Oh, c'mon now, don't hide back there. Let's have a look-see." She hopped down and put her shoes back on.

I yanked the bikini bottoms down in back and stepped out from behind the curtain, arms across my chest. My own bathing suit was a one-piece. "I don't know," I said. "Maybe I need a different size."

"Nonsense," said Trish. "There's no room for modesty around here, right Tim?" Tim looked at me and raised one eyebrow.

I backed carefully away, teetering in my new high heels. "They didn't say what kind of promo work I was supposed to be doing, and I've actually never worked at the Stampede before, so . . . " I looked down at my legs. Too bad the Stampede wasn't in August 'cause by then I'd have a tan.

"Shhh. Quit worrying," said Trish. "You have fantastic boobs." She scrunched up the bright pink fabric so it gathered more and didn't cover up as much skin. She cupped a breast in each hand from underneath, squished them together, then tightened the strings around the back of my neck. "Let's work 'em."

Once, the lady at the fitting room in The Bay's Young Miss Department told me I had a lovely bosom, but she didn't cup or squeeze them. She had said I should support them. Not "work 'em."

I followed Trish through the curtain opposite Tim's room to another metal door.

"Okay, this is where you go in and out. Now, git. Reggie's already there. Just do what he says. Let the people look at you. You're fifteen minutes on, five minutes off. Twenty minute break for dinner. Go straight to the break room when Reggie says. Whatever you do, don't speak out there. Just smile." She flashed her teeth at me. As if I didn't know how to smile.

"Oh, wait." She whipped out a tube of lipstick and dragged it across my mouth. I smacked my lips together, copying her. "That-a-girl. You look like Farrah Fawcett. Knock 'em dead."

I had written on my application that I was a quick learner. It was true. Grade nine was a cinch for me. People like Judy and Laura did hours of homework each night and struggled to get their sixty percent average. Big whoop. They hated that I got on the honour roll without even trying. And look how easy it was for me to get hired too! Dad said I must have been born with a horseshoe up my butt.

I took a deep breath and looked down. There was a cleavage line between my breasts that made them look bigger than normal. Was this slutty? Oh well. Didn't matter. It was my *job* now. I pushed the heavy trailer door open and there was Reggie, like some game show host or fancy magician.

"Aha! There she is!" He clapped a few times and waved an arm towards me. "Let's welcome my lovely assistant, Candy!" A few people whistled.

I looked behind me. Back at Reggie. "Katherine!" I mouthed.

He glared at me. I didn't want to get fired on my first day so I smiled back. "Right this way, Candy!" he said. I wobbled to the middle of a platform that was our stage. People riding the Tidal Wave screamed and music thumped from the Spinning Teacup. Reggie took my hand and spoke to the small crowd as if he were preaching to thousands.

"You may think Candy looks pretty sweet. Just the kind of girl you want to keep locked up all for yourself. But this juicy filly has a reputation as an escape artist. So I'm going to make sure she stays put while I tell you about the Human Oddities Show! Eight tickets and you can see them all! Next tour starts in just ten minutes! More freaks of nature than you've ever seen in one place!" People didn't stop eating their cotton candy or their popcorn or munching their snow cones when they walked by, but most at least looked over at us.

"Now, Candy, step this way," said Reggie pointing to a T-shaped metal bar on the opposite side of the stage. It looked like a cross, or a tall plus sign. It was difficult to straighten my legs as I walked. I wanted to tug at the crawling bikini bottom again, but that would have been embarrassing, so I let it crawl.

He guided me right in front of the cross.

"Arms up, baby-cakes," he ordered, loud enough so everyone could hear.

I raised both arms. It's harder to breathe with your arms over your head. "Whoa. Not so high! She's a frisky one, isn't she folks?"

I lowered them to straight out to the sides. He grabbed one of my wrists and pressed it against the horizontal part of the bar, a little on the rough side maybe.

"And now with this sturdy rope — " he showed the audience a piece of thick white rope, like a skipping rope but not as long " — I will bind Candy to this solid metal post."

He tucked his microphone under his arm so he had two hands to wrap the rope around my wrist and tie me to the bar. My other arm just hung in the air, looking dorky I'm sure. He made a big deal of pulling the rope tight, huffing and puffing as he tightened the ends to make sure the knot wouldn't come loose. It didn't hurt.

"Next," he ordered, and I gave him my other arm. He tied that wrist to the pole on the opposite side. It was more comfortable once both arms were tied up. He bent his head close to my cheek and I couldn't turn away from the audience. His moustache scratched my ear lightly and the heat from his breath went down the side of my neck.

"There's a snap in each rope," he wet-whispered. "At the back. You exert any pressure, and the ropes will fall right off. That's how you get free, okay? Don't move until you hear my cue." I kept smiling and tried to remember if I'd shaved my armpits. It was too late to check.

More people gathered near the stage. Reggie double-checked the knots against the pulse part of my wrists. "Nothing like a little bondage to keep a girl in her place," he said to the small crowd, and laughed.

He covered the microphone with one hand and told me to spread my legs apart. "A little further," he whispered. "Yes. That's it."

Then he started pacing back and forth in front of me with giant strides, talking about the attractions inside: the fattest man in the world, a yodelling midget, a man who could light himself on fire without getting burned. And much, much more.

"Step right up, ladies and gentlemen, for the Human Oddities Show. You've never seen anything like it! It'll take your breath away! A woman who swallows swords of steel! A girl who twists her leg around her own throat! Imagine that!"

All I had to do was stand there. Kind of like Jesus on the cross, but without thorns or nails, so it wasn't like it was hard work or anything. I kept thinking I might see Judy or Laura in the audience. Oh my God, if they saw me, they'd spaz out. They'd try and make me laugh. Laura would make that face and I wouldn't be able to even look. Maybe they'd go in and see Tim and the other freaks of nature. They could tell me about the ones I'd missed. I shifted from side to side; I was not used to these heels. My shoulders were getting a bit tired, but I didn't want to rest any weight on the ropes because I was afraid they might unsnap before it was time. People looked at me and I smiled the same smile the whole time. Kind of a squint. Wind blew hair in my face now and then, but there was nothing I could do about it. I just spat out the pieces that went in my mouth. I'm sure everyone wondered how I'd get free from the ropes. I started adding up the number of hours I was going to work that day, times $3.75, say $4, to make it easier. Seven hours per day, times how many days left of Stampede? I wondered if they'd pay me for the breaks, or if that was deducted at the end. I looked at the guy working the Lucky Horse game across the way. I looked at the clouds.

"And now, Candy, my delicious assistant, will release herself from bondage. Candy?" Reggie motioned to me, and I yanked my arms forward. I felt a little *click* and the ropes fell apart easily in the back and dropped to the stage floor. Easy-peasy. Just like he said. Reggie picked them up and swung them in big lasso circles before the crowd.

"Let's have a big hand for Candy!" People clapped. A few guys whistled. "Isn't she something?" said Reggie. More whistling. Someone shouted, "I'll eat you, Candy!" I felt about eighteen.

Trish was welcoming some people at the entry gate next to the stage, taking their tickets, and guiding them into the burgundy and velvet people-museum. Most of the crowd just walked away. A few old guys stood there staring.

Reggie did the "off you go" motion with his hand. "Eight tickets buys you the greatest display of human freaks ever seen!" he said as I left. Once I was out of view, I tugged the bikini bottoms down and went back to the room with the lockers. No one was there, so I peeked into the mini fridge. There were a few beer in there. Maybe we'd all sit around after and drink beer. Maybe I'd have one too. Why not? I plopped into a chair and flipped through magazines. I could hear people in the corridor and I imagined them gawking into the curtained rooms. Eight tickets. I wondered if that was a deal — looking at weirdos for eight tickets — compared with the other things you could do on the midway. Roller coaster was twelve. Forbidden Palace of Horrors was six. I drank the Five Alive from my backpack. If they paid me cash, I could do a ride after my shift before I had to meet Dad. If I had time.

Trish came in and said break time was over. She led me back to the stage door. "You're a natural out there. Just don't slouch. What's the point of having these if you don't show them off?" She adjusted my top again, put another layer of lipstick on me, patted me on the bum, and out I went.

"Well, looky looky!" said Reggie, acting surprised to see me. "It's my lovely assistant Candy. Right this way, Candy." The midway seemed busier; some people, the old guys, were still there from before. Reggie led me to the Jesus bar, made a big deal of calling me a restless filly, and tied my wrists up again. He was sweaty. I wasn't acting like a restless filly. I wasn't acting like anything. I wondered if I should; if they would like me better.

Standing there listening to him rave about the Human Oddities, I thought about whether I could get another kind of promo job after the Stampede. Maybe go up to Edmonton for Klondike Days in a few weeks. On to Vancouver for the PNE. Now that I had experience, I could travel all summer as a promo girl! The crowd gathered as I stood there. I remembered not to slouch. I wondered: if I stood up straighter would it make more people buy tickets to see a fat man or a bendy woman? If a record number of people bought tickets tonight, would I get a bonus? Can a promo girl get a promotion?

On cue, I pulled my arms free of the ropes and Reggie clapped. The people cheered, the suckers. It wasn't even magic. We sure were working it.

Another break, another coat of lipstick, another trip through the metal door to be tied to the cross. I made a point in my mind not to look directly at anyone. It wasn't about eye contact, this job. People were getting rowdier as the happy hour gang rolled out of the casinos and bars and onto the midway. Some people walked by without stopping. They just looked. Someone threw an empty slushie cup on the stage and it rolled to my feet. I kept smiling and kicked it away. I'd earned almost nine dollars now, if you counted from when I'd first arrived.

Then I saw them. The sun was low and shining in my eyes, but I knew it was them. Judy and Laura, together with Dad, walking by the Forbidden Palace of Horrors. What was he doing here?

I needed to cover up.

I needed to cover up like you need to close your eyes when you sneeze. Everything started rolling inside my belly. I started shivering. There was a sour taste in my mouth. I thought I might collapse, ropes or no ropes. Dad and Laura were talking and laughing, and Judy was carrying a big stuffed frog. I had to get out of there. I pulled my arms forward. The ropes fell. I clunked across the stage, looking down.

Reggie didn't miss a beat and he didn't come after me. "The Amazing Candy! Let's give her a big round of applause!"

The metal door slammed behind me just after someone yelled, "I'll lick your sweet ass, Candy!" In the break room, I kicked the heels off and pulled on my clothes over the bikini, hiked my backpack over one shoulder, and shoved the back door open.

I ran over extension cords, popcorn, and beer cans. A mouse scampered out of a pile of hamburger wrappers. Well, I thought, I could kiss those nine bucks goodbye, that's for sure. I didn't care. All I wanted was a shower.

I wondered if the sword swallower's dad ever came to the show. If the bendy woman's best friends knew where she worked. If Tim had sisters.

Just beyond the Employees Only gate I saw them again, partly hidden by a crowd of metalheads with Judas Priest and Metallica logos on their jean jackets. Dad, with my two best friends, hanging out, like it was a regular day at the Calgary

Stampede. They were heading to the Tilt-A-Whirl. I took a deep breath, redid my ponytail, hopped the gate and slid into step behind them.

"Hey guys!" I tried to be casual.

They all turned around. "Kath! You found us. Look at Froggie. Isn't he cute?" Judy wiggled the stuffed animal in front of my face. "Your dad won him!"

Dad put his arm over my shoulder. "No luck with the job hunt, eh?" I looked down and shook my head. "Well, the Grievers called. They want you to babysit tomorrow night." He took my chin in his hands. "You okay?"

Laura jumped in. "Oh my God. Nice lipstick. Hey, wanna barf? We're doing the Tidal Wave after this one. And there's an awesome Freak Show back there. They've got a guy who weighs like 900 pounds! Your dad says its exploitation, but I'm like, whatever."

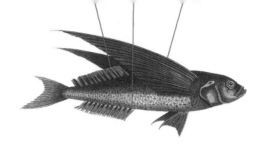

BLK MGC

IF YOU'RE LOOKING FOR EMILY, I can't help you.

She was in deep, Em. I didn't know how deep, at the time. How serious. Not until the end, and then it was too late. I found out more of the story later. From her ex, Norm. Peyton's dad. He said she'd had a few good months, when she first signed up. Made some money. Got her very own website. A free canvas briefcase was sent to her. So she went to the higher level. Upped her commitment. Upped her risk. He said she did it all wrong, Norm did. Too last minute. He said she didn't do her research. But you know Norm, always has to do things "just so". I figure that must have been when it all started going sideways and whatever happened in the parking lot happened.

That was the day she called me up to meet her after her kid was asleep.

"It's not a pyramid scheme," she tells me over a couple of honey crullers and coffee at Nell's All-Niter. She squishes her cigarette into the ashtray. She has Band-Aids on four different fingers and her hair's frizzled and knotted, like she slept on it wet and had bad dreams. A real mess, she is.

"How long have we known each other?" she asks me in that scratchy voice of hers. "You think I'd get involved in some goddamn pyramid scheme? All right, aside from the laundry balls thing? And maybe that business with the lottery tickets? No. Look. That was ages ago. Forget that. This is network marketing. Totally legit. It's the wave of the future, the new economy, and I want to share my good fortune with you."

She lights up another one, glances at her watch, and scans the diner.

"Trust me," she says, and I'm thinking she's real nervous. She's always been an edgy person, but ever since she stopped using, she'd calmed right down. Except that night. Things were different. So I'm like, she must be using again. And I wonder if she's in the mood to share, 'cause I could really use a hit. But I keep that idea to myself.

"Even Norm's on board." She says this because Norm's straight as a tack and if it's okay with Norm it's usually safe as sandwiches. We used to call him Normal Normie. He's the kind of guy who keeps paying his child support even though it's obvious she blows the whole wad on smokes and bingo, etc.

But still.

"I don't know," I says, checking out the place. There's only us there and a lady in all black with this weird hood on, sitting by herself in one of the corner booths. I have my back to her, but I know she's there 'cause we passed her when we came in and now I can hear her singing or murmuring something low. She has a funny smell. Not BO. More spicy. Like that Caribbean chicken you can get.

"It sounds great," I says, "but five hundred dollars? Who's got that kind of money?"

"I'm not denying that it's a significant amount of investment," she says, slow and bankerish. She leans in and whispers to me.

"This is only for people who are serious about earning money. Like, I mean super-serious. That's why I called you. Listen. When I first joined, I had to borrow pretty much all of it from Megan. Remember her? Well, I paid her back within two months. Two months! That's how long it took. I knew right away that it was a golden opportunity. Norm wasn't so sure at first. You know how he is. Cautious. Anyhow after three months I showed Megan my commission cheque and she couldn't believe it. Of course, she joined — at the Platinum Level — and next thing you know she's earning so much she doesn't know how to spend it." She tips back her chair like a big shot. "Literally does not know how." The waitress comes by and refills our cups.

"See her?" Em nods towards the woman lurching away from us with a coffee pot in one hand and a dishrag in the other. "What do you figure? Mid-fifties? Making minimum wage? She's tired. She's miserable. Pays rent with tips from this shitty job that just helps someone else get rich." She clicks her tongue, which says how pathetic it all is.

"You know her?" I says.

"That's not the point, okay?" She talks through clenched teeth. "I'm making a positive change in my life. No more rat race for me. I'm over it. And I want you to be with me in this. I don't want either of us to end up like her."

I don't mention that at least the waitress has a jay-oh-bee, but she seems to read my mind.

"I'm working for myself now. I'm my own boss. Making things good for Peyton and me. It's not cheap raising an eight-year-old these days, you know." She looks at her watch, then points to the clock over the fire extinguisher and yells to the waitress. "Hey! Is that the right time?"

"Yeah. 11:50. But don't worry, we're open all — "

"Okay," she says turning back to me. "Let's cut the bullshit. Are you in or what?"

"In? But I'm no good at selling stuff," I tell her. "I'm not confident, like you."

"YES YOU ARE!" she yells and looks over my shoulder to where the hooded lady is sitting. Then in a lower voice like she's talking to a four-year-old, "Yes. You. Are. Besides, it's barely even selling. You just tell your friends about it and they see you making money, you start driving a nice car, you start taking nice trips, and they say, 'Hey, sign me up!' and wham-bam-thank-you-ma'am you've got yourself that month's new member. Cash your cheque. Watch it grow. A friggin' empire."

"So I have to sign other people up? Give them the whole sales pitch?"

"It's not a sales pitch. It's sharing your story."

"My story?"

"They're gonna be banging on your door to sign up."

"Did they bang on your door?"

"You did, didn't you?"

"Well, actually, you called me."

"See? There's the old confidence! I knew you could. So. You've got a credit card, right?"

I do but it's maxed. She doesn't care and is talking faster and faster.

"Doesn't matter. I only need the number. We'll work out the details and shit later. And the expiry date, I'll need that too. Where's your wallet. Get your wallet. You brought your wallet right?"

My head's kind of spinning and I want to bum a smoke from her. She reaches across the table and takes my hands. Gently at first, but then squeezes pretty hard. She's showing me that she cares about my personal feelings. Her hands are wet and warm and shaking.

"Just give me your Visa card. You won't be sorry." She flashes a smile, then unflashes it. "This is about Peyton's future. You want my kid to have a future, don't you?" She reaches into her canvas briefcase and pulls out a fancy pen and some kind of legal contract with that same logo on the top. The hooded lady gets up. She's in this black skirt. I figure she must be pretty old from the way she's walking, wobbly and slow. A few chunks of nasty matted black hair hang down on the front of each shoulder, like dogs' tails. I can't see her face because of shadows. She's still humming. A bit crazy, but not the homeless kind. Em doesn't look at her — or me — when she brushes past our table.

I try being nice, 'cause she is one of my oldest friends and I don't want to make her feel bad. I tell her I'll think about it and that a new car and nice trips and a canvas briefcase and all the other frills sound appealing but that I have to head home because it's getting late. The bell on the door jingles as the old lady walks out. Wind whooshes in and a stack of receipts blows off the counter. I thank Em for the advice and am about to put my coat on when she practically leaps across the table and starts talking super close to me in a really harsh voice with lots of spit-spray. The whites of her eyes aren't very white at all. More yellow, with red veins. I can tell she hasn't slept for days. She's holding the pen in her fist and she's pointing it at me like she might write on my neck.

"You have to!"

"What?" I pull back.

"You have to. I can't tell you why. You just have to sign up. Right now. I need you to do it."

"Let go of me. God." I'm thinking, what's the big hairy deal. Take a chill pill. "I'd love to help you out, Em, but I'm not sure network marketing is my thing. I want to go home and Google it. I can't just give you my — "

"I thought I could count on you," she snarls. "I thought we were fucking friends."

She looks at the clock and inhales. Out the window I notice the hooded lady standing under a street light in Nell's All-Niter parking lot. She's holding something in one hand above her head. It's shaped like a big gingerbread man. Or a doll. She has it by the leg and she's kind of shaking it. There's this bandana wrapped around the thing's head, like the one Peyton always used to wear when he played pirates. Her other hand is raised up in the air too. Her mouth is moving but the top half of her face is all shadowed. She looks way taller out there than she did in the diner. She's swaying like there's slow music on. Her skirt is blowing to one side and I hadn't noticed before how long it was.

"Em. Check it out," I says, completely forgetting what we were talking about. "Check out that freaky woman outside."

She grabs my arms. With both hands. Way too tight.

"Please! Just sign this! It's about Peyton!"

"Hey. Em. Calm down," I tell her in a social worker voice. "Peyton will be fine. You're having a bad trip. That's all. What did you take? Tell me what you took."

"Christ. Nothing. You don't understand." She presses her fists on her forehead. Her face is almost purple. She's shaking and looking back and forth between me and the psycho lady out the window. Then she lets out this noise, this screech, like she's giving birth or something. The waitress and the cook stop what they're doing.

"You were my only hope!" she bellows and darts out the door. I kind of freeze. Last thing I hear is those bells. Waitress is bent down picking up the receipts again. She shakes her head and gives me one of those *I've seen it all* looks.

I'm thinking, holy shit that's messed up. I lay a five on the table, put on my coat and head out after her, but by the time I get out there she's gone. So's the old lady. All's I find is this doll. And this bandana. And this long pin.

So, no. I don't know where Emily is.

I do see Peyton now and then. Cute kid. Doesn't say much though. He walks with a limp and he has this weird scar below one eye. He's living with Normal Normie these days. I hear Norm took over Em's business accounts and signed up a few of his friends and neighbours and they signed up a few of their friends and neighbours. You know how it goes. I don't regret not signing up. Some people have a knack for network marketing. Not me.

Word is, Norm's got a girlfriend now too. Some older lady. From Jamaica. Maybe Barbados. Anyhow, just last week I saw him driving a new car with the license BLK MGC. He had his elbow resting out the window and was whistling a tune I knew I'd heard before somewhere.

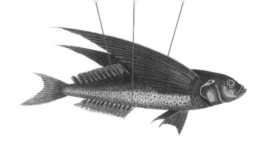

Cannonball

"Luke, we have to talk," she says.

We're on our way to the pool for Public Swim, and she's been quiet until now. She's driving cautiously, stopping at orange lights and crosswalks. I figure something's up. She puts out her cigarette in the ashtray between our seats. I know I'll be able to breathe better soon.

"Yeah?" I say. With her, I know it won't be talk like as in having a conversation. That kind of talk, ping-pong style, back and forth, that isn't so bad. That I can do. Like with me and Carma. But Mum's "we have to talk" means she wants to unload about how tired she is of doing everything around the house or lecture me about setting an example for the twins or discuss sexuality and how normal my feelings are or how I have to pull up my grades. "We have to talk" means I have to listen and she doesn't want to hear what I have to say even if I were to come right out and say it.

"There's something important I have to tell you," she says.

I bet she's gay. Like Yardley's mom. That would explain a lot. Dad'll need therapy. It's probably Wilma from the library. I'll have to call one Mum and one Mother. I knew it. It'll be weird at first but maybe things will settle down and there will be less fighting and better meals. Or — second thought — what if she hacked into my computer and knows about those sites me and Carma go to? She'll put up a firewall. Or change the password for a week without internet. No, she'd be more mad. She said "Something important." So it's not a mad thing. Maybe she has cancer. Her voice is crackly like someone who has throat cancer and is going to lose their hair. Who will raise me if she goes bald and dies? I'll have to get a suit for the funeral. Black. I'll be an orphan. One of those older orphans that never get adopted. But I guess there's still Dad. Maybe it's about Dad. Maybe he's gotten a job. That would shake things up. Or what if she's pregnant? I think she might be pregnant again. She has gotten quite fat lately. Dad's noticed too. That would totally suck. Me and the twins are enough. Or maybe it's something good-important. Maybe she finally sold a painting. Maybe she got picked up by a big city gallery like she's always talking about. Or we won a trip to Disneyland. I could handle Disneyland. I could not handle another baby in the house. Or wearing a black suit to a funeral.

"Okay," I say, very cool, as we drive past WalMart and Home Depot and Staples and Payless Shoes. Carma will think I'm too old to go to Disneyland, but if I invite her to come with us, she'll change her tune pretty quickly. They have fireworks every single night in Disneyland. Mom takes a deep breath. I notice out of the corner of my eye that she has pulled her lips inside her mouth so it looks like a scar in the middle of her face.

"You're going to have to be very grown-up about this," she says.

Not good. This is not a good thing for an eleven-and-three-quarters-year-old to hear. They don't tell you you have to be very grown-up and then tell you "pack your bags, kiddo, we're going to Disneyland!" They tell you you have to be very grown-up about things that little kids can't handle. Relationship things. Death. Maybe somebody died. Maybe Grandpa died. Maybe someone who was going to die didn't die. Or someone who has already died has come back to life. What if she actually died in her sleep last night and now has come back as a zombie. It happens in Africa all the time. It could happen here.

"This isn't easy for me," she says, tapping her fingers on the steering wheel. I bet they're getting a divorce. That's probably it. That's the kind of thing that isn't easy because divorces are messy. I'll live with Dad on weekends and Mum during the week. Dad'll take the checkered couch no matter where he gets his condo. Carma gets two allowances and two Christmases and says it's way better except when her dad is late picking her up. Then it can get ugly, she says. I keep looking out my window. I see smudges and fingermarks, some bird crap, a smeared mosquito.

"Are you listening, Luke?" Oh, she knows I'm listening. I have no choice. The car is small. She's all voice. She lights up another cigarette, drives with her knees. Mom's either dying or we're going to Disneyland or she's become a zombie and I don't know what's going to happen next. We're in the parking lot now and there's only forty-five more minutes of Public Swim left. Carma's going to be waiting and she doesn't like waiting.

"Uh-huh," I say. I don't want to seem like I don't care but if she has cancer or we're having another baby I wish she'd just tell me and get it over with because you know what they say: life goes on. I really don't want to miss my whole swim.

"You know I love you." This is the thing she says before she says something that says the exact opposite. It is usually followed by "but" or "and this is for your own good".

I put my hand on the door handle. I want out. There's no air in here, with all this talk and smoke.

"I'm leaving," she says. I don't know if she means *leaving* leaving or just leaving. I want to ask what she's talking about and when she's coming back and where leaving goes and who exactly is she leaving behind, but she did say I was going to have to be grown-up and grown-ups don't ask so many questions.

"Yeah?" This time I look at her. Right in the eyes. But they are teary so I don't look anymore.

"It's so complicated, honey," she says, shaking her hair back and putting her hands against her temples. Her breathing shakes.

I want to hug her but instead I just look at her for one more sec, grab my backpack, run out of the car, and slam the door without meaning to. Out of breath, I put my shorts on in the men's room, where the lockers fall towards me and the chlorine smell twists up my stomach. I scan the pool for Carma. She's next in line for the Tarzan swing. My best friend, wearing that bikini.

"Hey, Luke!" she yells and waves at me. "Over here!"

I plug my nose and cannonball into the deep end. My hair rises up like seaweed as I slowly sink to the bottom of the pool where I sit until my lungs run out of air.

The Siren Sisters

(No. 18): *I choose to accept that which cannot be changed.* I repeat this over and over in my head, but I still can't fall asleep. It's like a movie that plays on the inside of my eyelids. The four of them in that boat, just before it capsized. The screams. Hands grabbing for ropes. Someone's hat. A boot. Yesterday's Daily Affirmation (No. 17): *I allow my feelings to ebb and flow, without overanalyzing them.* I have fifty I rotate through. At first you just want to indulge in tears and give in to the darkness, but eventually the words start to sink in. They are the only way I have to deal with my feelings of guilt, uncertainty, loss, and the pressure to be perfect. Affirmations have always been part of my life, but after what happened last Monday, I need them more than ever.

This week's been a bitch and I've relapsed four times. My sisters still aren't talking to me. They say I stole their futures and they blame me for everything. I feel like shit but there's no reasoning with them. Things are still too raw and the tension's as thick as honey. Phone has been driving everyone batshit, doing scales and arpeggios non-stop; her emotional outlet. Thexie hasn't so much as brushed her teeth since the accident. She tends to ride the crazy train whenever there's no sailor for her to fix, but of course this week it's worse than ever and the empty bottles have been piling up all over the island.

Obviously I'm not pleased with the way things went, but I *am* confident that we're on the right course. I know in my heart it was what Dad wanted too. Everything in the universe happens for a reason. Still, I wish we could go back to the way things were. Way, way back.

I suppose there is an innate conservatism in being the oldest sibling. It's probably because we first-borns subconsciously want to return to the good old days of being an only child, a being whose every burp was celebrated with a festival or the commissioning of a new tune for the lyre. My glory days didn't last long. A year to be exact, and a year after that, there were three of us. That's when the legend begins.

Phone is the baby of the family. Dad used to say she's the most like Mother of all of us. (Obviously not physically: Phone has muscular arms and hardly any cellulite — Polyhymnia was at least twenty-five pounds overweight her whole life, even though I swear I don't remember her eating anything thicker than a vine leaf.)

Thexie is the middle sister. Thelxiepeia is her real name, but try saying *that* with a mouthful of feta. If we lived on the mainland, Thexie would probably be one of those bleeding-heart-stray-dog-adopting people. As it is, after every wreck, while Phone and I are down salvaging supplies, food, gear, galley appliances, or electronics that haven't been too damaged, Thexie fetches sailors. Traditionally, they all drown. But if there happens to be one who survives the skeleton-smashing waves through our jagged igneous rock outcroppings and crawls to our craggy, debris-strewn, crab-infested shore, Thexie's all *oh baby oh baby* and carries him up all ninety-eight stairs to the house, stems his bleeding, realigns his bones, and spoils him back to health and vigour.

Technically, we don't support this. Dad used to argue that all the sailors should be left alone to die — that's the way Mother would have wanted it. But after she took off, Dad kind of gave up in the discipline department. Whether it's lazy parenting or part of his fantasy about wanting to become a grandpa, he doesn't discourage Thexie's relationships. So I lay off too.

She does tend to drink a little less retsina when there's a wounded man to fawn over. And when the dude has recovered, the two of them have a therapeutic romp in the sack (or hammock, or olive net) before she sends him off — usually on a dodgy little raft made of wood pallets, rope, and bleach bottles — around the back of the island where it's safe. Generally the guy has a big shit-gobbling grin on his face as he bobs off through the waves, although who's going to believe that he was the only member of his crew to survive a shipwreck, was nursed back from death's door on an island most people don't even think exists, and fucked a siren before he left?

Phone, on the other hand, is not into wounded guys at all. We think her compassion gene went missing at birth. She is literally repulsed by the sight of blood, guts, bones, etc. She didn't even bother to help when Dad sprained his ankle after he leapt from the La-Z-Boy during a particularly rousing episode of *Storage Wars* a few months ago. What kind of a daughter won't put frozen sea-buckthorn berries on her own father's swollen foot? But does she brighten up once the scars are healing and Thexie's lucky sailor is up and walking? OMG. That's when she realizes the guy might be her ticket off of Anthemoessa, and she launches into heaving diva mode, hoping to impress him with her full soprano and deep cleavage. Hoping to pull a Kelly Clarkson and get "discovered." And if flirting with her sister's cause might help her *own* cause? Well, a girl has to do what a girl has to do.

There's lots to dislike about Phone. Not only is she the youngest, she also has big boobs, skinny thighs, and a flat belly. Her full name is Aglaophonos. She hates it when I call her Phone. But I hate it when she does vibrato. She wants to enroll in a dramatic arts academy. And not just in Athens. She wants to move to New York. Or LA. We're not surprised. She has always been a spotlight hog. While Thexie and I sing our warm-ups sweetly and gently, she's all in your face, "Don't cry for me Argentina", and so on. Our songs don't have words. They're just open vowels, like the wind and the whales and what comes out of seashells, but Phone will go all Celine Dion if I let her. She practises so hard she brought down a Cessna once. "Not kosher," scowled Dad, even though he pilfered a whole case of dry cigarettes from the wreckage.

Unless there's a boat to seduce and smash, things don't change much from day to day around here. We wake up with the sun (except when the night-vision alarm on the Ship-Trip Insta-Cam goes off, in which case we rush to cliff's edge in our PJs, eyes still full of sleep crud and burst into night song, the last notes the sailors will ever hear). Just coffee for me for breakfast, then vocal warm-ups at cliff's edge, so we can keep watch at the same time. We massage the sides of our jaws, recite "Loose Lips Sink Ships" ten times quickly, do the *ma may me mo mu* with slow exhales, then "Do-Re-Mi" forward and back and so on. I lead, because I always have. After lunch (which for me is usually a spinach salad with dressing on the side or a bit of brown quinoa, while Thexie and Phone pretty much eat whatever's in the fridge — recall No. 29: *I am proud of who I am and I resist the temptation to compare myself to those around me)*, the three of us just hang out in the meadow on the upper cliff, stringing flower chains, working on our tans, and scanning the horizon, while Dad sits inside and smokes and watches satellite TV.

Things aren't as busy as they used to be. Some people think we get a boat every day. But with all the fancy new navigational equipment, fewer and fewer vessels make the mistake of trying to come through the Anthemoessa Passage at all anymore. I'd say it's two boats per week, max.

But despite declining nautical traffic, there have been a string of fuck-ups recently. And with each one, Dad gets more and more stressed about the possibility of turning ninety. ("What's so great about being an immortal nonagenarian?") He takes it out by lecturing me and I take it out by bingeing and purging.

Party yachts are the worst. Luxury pleasure cruisers that have their own million dollar stereos cranked, blasting Lil Wayne and Ke$ha. We've had to project our voices like bloody vocal shot putters just to get their attention, and even so we did let two through recently. Then we figured out that as long as they get a good visual of us, they'll turn down their wretched sound systems and listen, just out of curiosity, *hee hee*, then *whoosh!* Boat down.

Most recently, it was the Belgian Tone Deaf Association's ship. We couldn't believe it when we saw the flag. Dad turned eighty-six when that friggin' boat made it through.

You see, every time a ship gets through, a year is added onto each of our lives. That's the deal. Otherwise, we're immortal.

Dad too. We were fourteen, fifteen and sixteen years old for nearly two idyllic, vessel-wrecking centuries. Dad put up a sign on the south side of Anthemoessa: "Check Out Our Record: 188 Years Non-Accident-Free!" Phone's like "Hello? Don't you think the billboard thing might depend on your perspective, Pops?" But Dad only has one perspective. I thought it was pretty cool too, so together we'd hike down there every New Year's morning to update it. On the way back I'd get to hear about how proud he was of his girls, of me for being such a good role model.

I'm the one who takes the heat, though, when a ship does pass safely. Dad brings us all into his chamber to give us "the talk," but it's me he glares at the whole time. We know what he's going to say. We bring dishonour to the family name. If Mother were around, she would not let this happen. We have a tradition to uphold. When is one of us going to give him a grandchild? (He always manages to squeeze that in, even though it has nothing to do with anything.) We aren't going to be immortal forever, not at this rate, yadda yadda. And he makes me lead choral exercises until our tongues are blue and our throats are raw.

Then I go raid the pantry.

The night of the Belgian Tone-Deaf Association incident I ate the inside of an entire loaf of sweet bread with honey, half a pan of moussaka, about two dozen Goldfish crackers dipped in Nutella, and a case of spring rolls we got off a sightseeing boat from Hong Kong. That night's affirmation happened to be No. 42: *A weak moment doesn't mean I am a weak person, or that my path cannot and will not change.* It seemed kind of hollow, but I repeated it over and over anyhow.

Glitches aside, I realize our life must seem idyllic: three (practically) forever-youthful sisters singing; elderly father relaxing his days away; scores of earthly treasures collected from centuries of shipwrecks. The sun, the meadow, the ocean views. Bliss. I watch CNN and I see what it's like out there. Environmental issues. Homelessness. Political turmoil. Kids on crack. But now and then I can understand how the tranquility of our life got under Mother's skin.

"A Muse is meant to *inspire*," I overheard her saying to Dad early one morning several years ago. "Not *kill*. I love you, Achelous, but I need to follow my dreams. The girls can do the luring on their own from now on. The world is my oyster and I intend to gulp it down." I hid in an alder bush and watched my father sob until her dinghy disappeared into the pastel horizon.

Dad's official explanation was that Mother was under a lot of stress and needed some me time. I found out from Aunt Terpsichore that she was eventually hired as a singer/dancer in Roger Rabbit's Dancing Time Warp at Tokyo Disneyland. She made craploads of yen for a few years, but of course she was aging like a common mortal so inevitably turned forty. When she was fired she started teaching Business English to employees at Toshiba in Osaka. Through Facebook I know she now lives in a penthouse apartment with Toshiba's Kansai district manager. They fly to Scotland for golf weekends and post photos of themselves in kilts. I don't tell this to Dad. And he doesn't get the deal with social media, which is good.

So you can imagine our surprise/shock/fear/excitement last week when a helicopter hovered over our island in the middle of the afternoon and three figures fell through the sky for a few moments, were caught by parachutes, and drifted down to our meadow like giant candy-coloured jellyfish. We rubbed our eyes

and strained our necks. When we realized we were not commu-
nally hallucinating, we did some hysterical shrieking and ran
inside. Dad was watching *Antiques Roadshow*. I grabbed a bag of
Doritos from the coffee table and started autopiloting them into
my mouth. Phone fixed her hair while Thexie bounced up and
down singing, "It's raining men, hallelujah!"

Ever since Mother left Dad's been almost completely agora-
phobic. Or, as Phone says, he's a lame-ass. He just sits inside
watching shitty American TV; if it isn't a reality show about
some morons and the crap they accumulate, he doesn't give a
flying fart. But when he peeked through the shutters with us
that day and saw three strangers unbuckling their buckles,
gathering up their parachutes, and gawking around our island,
well, farts flew.

"Sonofabitch," said Dad, just about spilling his iced coffee.
"Looks like we've got company."

There were two men and one woman. The woman was
already taking pictures with her phone, while the men laughed
and backslapped and waved their arms around like they were
showing each other the sights.

"Go see what they want, Peisinoe," said Dad, looking at me.
My mouth was too full to argue. "Girls. Go with Pins. But let
her do the talking." There was a tremor in the bag under his left
eye. He was scared.

Phone reapplied her lipstick, adjusted her tank top, pulled
her hairband out, and fluffed her curls. "Maybe they're talent
scouts," she said.

Thexie grabbed three Orange Fantas from the fridge. "Maybe
they're lost," she said.

I told Dad not to worry, we'd deal with it, and brought him a beer. "Maybe they're the Coast Guard and we're all under arrest and we're going to be hauled off to Athens and put on trial for the murder of thousands of mariners," I thought, but didn't say.

As we started up towards the meadow, I recalled the last time we'd interacted with healthy strangers. It had been only a few years earlier. Seems Salty Seas Co. was having a Barbershop Quartet Cruise. Since when do barbershop quartets need their own cruise? Can't they just sing in barbershops? Anyhow, we positioned ourselves right on cliff's edge and started singing as soon as we spotted the ship: melancholy, fatally irresistible, enchanting, the usual. And what happened? The crew and passengers joined right in! Started weaving tenor and bass harmonies all over our lines. The girls looked at me with big eyes like *WTF?* It was as if they were immune to our musical spell. I shrugged my shoulders like *Hey, why not? Let's go with it!* Trying to be Fun Big Sister. And we kept singing. We upped the ante with a nice crescendo, a key shift, and then we burst into a peppy staccato section. We were all snapping our fingers, getting right into it. And we sounded pretty good, I admit. It was kind of jazzy, kind of crazy, singing with men, bouncing melodies off each other across the waves. Then the cruise ship guys started doing some bluegrassy numbers. *O Brother, Where Art Thou?* stuff. I was thinking it's all okay because eventually the Salty Seas ship would get too close to the island, crash, and sink into the watery grave like the rest, so no harm done.

Then Phone started acting really weird. She inched closer to the cliff edge like she was hypnotized. She looked back at us, all twitchy, hair blowing in her face and said, "I can't resist! It's now or never!" Thexie and I stopped singing midphrase, but before we knew it, Phone had whipped off her sundress and taken a flying leap into the sea. One of the lesser gods must have been watching over her because somehow she didn't crack her skull open on a rock. But not even Zeus himself could help that landlubber swim. People get us mixed up with mermaids all the time (thank the Roman revisionists for that), but let me tell you we are about as buoyant as ceramic pots. I'm pretty sure her big tits were the only things that kept her from sinking to the bottom of the drink like a steel turd.

What gets me is that all those guys on the stupid a cappella boat (can I say fairy ferry?) *must* have seen her flailing around, and they didn't even throw her a lifering. They just segued into some jaunty Broadway show tunes, navigated the ship past my drowning sister, away from the deadly rocks, and made safe passage, the buggers. That's when we discovered how dangerous it can be for us to genre-swap. We'd let a Salty Seas cruise liner get through, *and* just about lost Phone.

Once we'd pumped the salt water from her lungs and plucked the kelp off of her she was fine. We all felt pretty stupid though, like we'd been suckered into letting a vessel pass just because the crew sang. Beat at our own game!

The parachuters waved as soon as they saw us.

"Friendly, anyhow," whispered Thexie. I reminded her not to be fooled so quickly.

The woman had a bit of cellulite in the triceps area and a muffin top hanging over unflattering yoga pants. I'd say she was about 130 pounds. Probably mid-thirties. Long straight black hair in a loose ponytail, a hint of grey roots. The men couldn't have been more different from each other. One was short, bald, and flabby, with a red shiny balloon face — he was walking beside the woman. The other, tall and lean, with a head of wavy grey hair, followed a few steps back. All three were smiling, fake and huge, like their teeth were too cold or something.

"The Siren Sisters!" It was baldy. "Can it be?" He reached his hand out but I did not extend mine. Phone moved to edge in front of me, but a quick elbow in the ribs put her back in her spot. "I can't believe it's really you," said the man. "In the flesh. The three of you. It is such an honour. I can't tell you. Such beautiful women, such enchantresses. Such legends!"

Such bullshit.

"Welcome to our island!" said Thexie, barrelling past me and handing each a Fanta. "You must be thirsty! We saw you parachute in. That was amazing! We were all like, 'That's amazing,' weren't we girls?"

"It's true. We were all so goll-dang amazed." Phone was speaking in a country-western accent.

"I'll handle this," I said, giving them both the squint. "This island is private property."

The sweaty fat man rubbed his hands together, like he was trying to decide his next move. The woman took a swig of her drink and swished it around before swallowing it loudly.

It was the tall guy from behind who piped up: "We have come to your island uninvited, and it has obviously caused distress. A thousand apologies for the intrusion." He did a little idiotic samurai warrior bow. Thexie's hand fluttered to her bosom.

What Greek worth his souvlaki doesn't know that "apology" comes from *apologetics — speaking in defense*? He wasn't sorry. I glared at him.

He attempted to look pleadingly at me, but one of his eyes drifted skyward and off to the right, like it was following a bird overhead. It threw me off, that wandering eye. "It's okay," I stammered, mostly to avoid looking at him.

"Yes. How rude of us. And to not even introduce ourselves." It was fatty again.

Apparently he was a head honcho on the Greek Tourism Board. Kris Liakakos or Thialakos. He tried to give me a card, but I kept my arms folded across my chest. Phone made a dramatic *plié* for the card, which she coyly stuffed into her bra. The woman was Twyla Hoop, a TV producer from NBC. American. And crazy-eye was Vince Valetti, a fancy-pants Italian real estate developer.

A micro-gasp escaped from Thexie. I thought she was going to sneeze, until she stepped forward and croaked: "Vinny? Vinny who got sliced in the ribs with the propeller? Vinny with the head injury? Is that you?"

"I didn't know if you'd recognize me," the crooked-eyed developer whined. "It's been nearly twenty-five years since the wreck of the *Marlin Monroe*." He pulled up his shirt and showed us a purple gash in his torso.

"Ew. Gross," said Phone, plugging her nose as if the scar stank.

"You saved my life, Thelxiepeia," said Vince. "Without you, I would have bled to death."

"I didn't think I'd ever see you again, Vinny," whimpered Thexie.

"I'm fifty years old now. But you. You are as lovely as ever. You haven't changed a bit!"

"Well, she has," I corrected. "A bit."

Hugging and fawning ensued.

"How's that for a Hollywood reunion?" said Twyla Hoop. "I'm gonna need a tissue."

I'm gonna need a barf bag, I thought. There is a reason we let them die. Besides being Greek tradition, it's a matter of clarity. Basic sanitation. It gets so messy when they live.

"So. What brings you back to our fair island, Vincent?" said Phone, now adopting a Julie Andrews *Sound of Music* tone. "If it's just for the sex, surely you didn't need an entourage." Faces reddened; fat Kris chuckled. "Or are you here to avenge the lives of your fellow sailors? The ones who weren't so lucky upon our rocky shores?"

"I harbour no ill feelings about what happened to the *Marlin*," said Vincent, tucking his polo shirt back in. "We knew the risks. We'd heard the stories. We were curious. We thought we could just listen for a moment, and yet we could not resist." He lowered his voice and we all leaned in. "I don't know quite how to describe it. For me, it was as if your siren harmonies perfectly matched the pitch of the fluids in my body. You sang the chemistry of my blood. Each note resonated like a song my body remembered from when I floated in my Mother's womb. Spiritual ambrosia. Aural heroin. We needed to hear more. Yes, your music was a drug, and we were junkies. We held the needle to our veins and listened. We made a fist, and listened. We pierced the skin, and listened. It wasn't the music that destroyed us. No, the music gave us power. It opened the universe. We did not want it to end. It was this urge for more that drove us to you. Never mind nautical hazards, eddies like tornadoes and waves crashing over rocks. You enchanted us, but we stoned ourselves. We threw ourselves onto your jagged altar. As experienced sailors, we only had ourselves to blame."

I'd never thought of it like that. I'd always kind of figured we were like genetically programmed killers. Like polar bears, with their natural instinct to kill the little seals. But no. We weren't polar bears after blood, necessarily. We were singers. Damn good ones too. It wasn't our fault they couldn't steer their boats. Does nice scenery cause car accidents?

I'm looking at him, thinking: this means that all those other sailors must have died happy. Like the guy who dies of heart failure having sex with his mistress. Is it *her* fault she's an awesome lay and he neglected to his keep his cholesterol in check?

"So." Kris cleared his throat. "We are here with a business proposition. As you know — well maybe you don't, sorry, I've never met a — well, anyhow, let me start again. Television network ratings have been falling. Tourism in Greece is at an all-time low, and the economy of the entire EU is basically in the crapper. Especially Greece."

Twyla finally spoke. "We've been looking for a way to take advantage of this window of opportunity. To synergize our collective goals — entertainment, tourism, and land development. So we've formed this little tiger team. Vince? Kris? Shall we open the kimono?"

"I've got goosebumps!" said the pushover-siren. Thexie linked her arm through Vince's. "But Dad's gonna wanna hear all about it. Let's go up to the house."

As we walked up the meadow path, Phone saddled up to Twyla Hoop. "I've always favoured NBC over any other network. Your arts programming is *unsurpassed*. Your coverage of the death of Whitney Houston brought me to tears." It was all the segue she needed to burst into "I Will Always Love You."

I wondered how exactly we were going to get rid of them. Dad wouldn't have the time of day for their synergy and tiger teams and open kimonos. He's not interested in business deals or marketing people. Aside from TV, Dad has three obsessions: the shit that washes up on shore (you should see our shed!), preserving Greek tradition, and, most fervently, becoming a grandpa. He thinks if there were little ones on the island, Mother would come back. "Your mother always wanted to be a granny," he says. "You girls get yourselves pregnant and have some cute little *eggonia* that I could bounce on my knee, your mother would be here before you could say Aphrodite's Nightie, mark my words. We'd be a whole family again." He says he'd tell them stories about their ancestors, living and dead. Mother would teach them to bake, sew, garden. Then his eyes juice up, his chin quivers, and he stares into the middle distance. "She was a good gardener, my Polyhymnia was. Those fig trees didn't just plant themselves, you know."

It's not going to happen. Not her coming back, and certainly not one of us having a baby. You try carrying a fetus to term when you're immortal. The biology is impossible. If *you* don't age nine months, how can you expect an *embryo* to develop? Ask Thexie. That girl's as fertile as the Nile Delta — she gets knocked up by pretty much every sailor who passes through her panties — but never carries past first trimester.

"Snap out of it, old man," Phone said to him recently with all the compassion of an eggplant. "For you to be a granddaddy, we'd have to give up everything. Go mortal. Hello? The lifespan of the average Greek male is only seventy-seven, no matter how much olive oil you cook with. You're already living on borrowed time." Dad shrugged his shoulders. Said he's had a full life over the past however-many centuries and is ready to move on. Said he's bored. Said having some kids around here, and Mother back too, would be just the send off into the afterlife he wants. "Besides, with grandchildren, I'd be immortal in a different kind of way."

"Offspring? Screw that," Phone told me later. "For me, true immortality means having a single on the Billboard Top Ten."

When the six of us arrived at the house, the TV was muted on *Hoarders*, and even though it was the middle of the afternoon the wine bottle candles were lit. Dad had even removed his *Keep Calm and Sail On* ball cap and smoothed his remaining hair across his forehead. "Sausage roll?" he said. "Fried won tons? Mini quiche?" Our father had, in the thirty minutes since we'd left him, defrosted and neatly arranged more food than he'd prepared since the first Olympics.

Twyla did most of the talking: "I'll just give you the thumbnail. It's a multi-faceted project, all 110 percent hush-hush — I had to pull a few strings in Accounting just to get this far, but when Vinny and Kris agreed to come on board, I knew we had a rocket brigade. We brainstormed outside the box, ran the numbers, and we've come up with a win-win proposal that will knock your socks off. Something that is going to take the entertainment world *and* the tourism industry by the tighty-whities and give them a giant feel-good wedgie."

Kris butted in to clarify now and then, while Vince looked googly-eyed at one or perhaps both of my sisters.

In a nutshell, the Greek government had sold the island (our island!) to Olive Grove Development Co. (Vince's business), who, along with Tourism Greece and NBC Studios, had concocted a new reality TV show called *Snag-A-Siren*, involving teams of three men (Americans, one would assume) battling the elements to reach the source of the world's most seductive singers.

"*Snag-a-Siren*? Are you kidding me?" I said.

"Don't interrupt, Pins," said Thexie, a piece of hair twirled around her finger. "I think it sounds kinda cute. Go on, Twyla."

The program was to be a Greek isle combination of *Survivor* and *The Bachelor*. *X Factor* meets *Wipeout* with Hellenic flair. And the winning trio would take us on an all-expenses paid "date."

"So as you three sing your little hearts out on the cliff, the brave challengers will sail through all kinds of nautical hazards. We'd get our best people to design an obstacle course with plastirocks, fake shipwrecks poking out of the water, mechanical sharks, that kind of thing. We'd of course have to use a safe section of the island — "

"The east side," said Thexie. "That's where you'll want to be."

"Right. You know what happens when Insurance and Legal get together."

"Sure do!" said Thexie, not looking at me.

"Then, the winning team would meet you on the island and there'd be a campy who-likes-who segment, maybe some frolicking on the beach time while you get to know each other. Some sisterhood rivalry. Some macho drama. Then the three couples are off for a romantic "date" in Paris, New York, Rio. You name it. But it only happens if the sisters agree who is with whom. That's part of the fun. Each of you chooses your own Aegean Hero." Twyla did air quotes on the Aegean Hero part.

"Actually we're thinking the date will be on Santorini," said Kris. "Or Mykonos."

Twyla pulled a laptop out of her bag. "Anyhow. I know it's a lot to swallow, so I've done up a video infographic. Don't worry, the actors, cameramen — everyone on set — signed non-disclosure contracts." She pressed play. Three actresses (who looked *nothing* like us) wearing these billowy rayon dresses (that my sisters and I wouldn't wear to clean fish in) stood on a rock outcrop singing (flat) to teams of boats (wow — do they still make Lasers?) that had to navigate their way through a (lame) slalom course.

Kris explained that they wanted to create a mysterious/sexy Siren Sisters "brand" to lure people to the island to watch live tapings of the show ("But, um, without killing them," Vince interjected. He and Thexie shared a laugh). This, in exchange for what Twyla called an *outrageously* generous compensation package for us.

"Oh, and we are actually going to let go of the term 'lure', remember, Kris?" said Vince.

"International?" said Phone.

"Of course," said Twyla. "You'll be like the Greek Kardashians."

Phone grabbed my forearm. Her palm was sweaty.

"We'd also like to apply to have your home preserved as a World Heritage Site," said Kris. I thought of the shed, bursting with crap we'd dragged up over the years. "It will be a global honour for the island. For your family." Right. A lot of good "global honour" had done for the Peloponnesians in Olympia. I took my sixth sausage roll, dipped it in the honey-mustard, and eyed the last mini quiche.

"Essentially," said Twyla, "we are still at concept, but at the end of the day we are looking to empower *you* with this proposal. We don't need a yay or a nay at this exact moment in time — of course you're going to want to bounce this around — talk to your lawyer, your accountant — but we want to plant the seed and fertilize it with some positive momentum."

I'd been waiting for Dad to tell them to get the hell off his island, or for Thexie to take her hand off Vince's knee and slap him with it, or for Phone to call them all amateurs and explain that we were better than some cheesy reality show. I waited for someone to say that we had a tradition to uphold. Tell them to go read their fucking Classics. I waited for a lightning bolt from one of our relatives to crack through the ceiling, reminding us of the immortality clause. Of our *duties*. But when I looked at each of their faces I saw sparkles. The biting of lips, the gleeful clasping of hands.

A red light on the Insta-Cam next to the microwave started flashing. Dad raised one eyebrow and cleared his throat. "Girls?" He nodded out the window to the horizon and the mood collapsed.

It was a little fishing boat. We dashed out the door and started singing before we even reached cliff's edge. My gut was bloated from all those greasy hors d'oeuvres. What I really needed was to hit the loo, but the boat was already safely past Bedlam Belt and was crossing Satan's Spire. Our music was off-pitch and no one was breathing quite right, but we kept going, switched keys and slowed things down until finally our song began to fall into place. After a few minutes, I noticed Dad and the three assholes watching us sing from behind the almond tree like children playing spies, and I overheard things like *worldwide opportunity, wasted talent, embrace change,* and *carry on the family name.*

Down below, four fishermen, overdressed for the weather like fishermen always are, leaned against the rails of their boat and strained their necks. Like they wanted to fly out of their boats to reach us. Like heaven was only slightly out of reach.

Once we found our groove, we elevated our voices in a velvety crescendo, with rich harmonies that even gave *me* the shivers. Maybe it was the adrenalin from sprinting, maybe it was having an audience of strangers who we weren't intent on killing, or maybe it was because that damn boat got halfway through and we had to totally pour it on to prevent them from gaining safe passage.

I looked at Phone — her eyes shut, lost in the ecstasy of the music — and I started to wonder. Was her gift indeed being wasted on ears of the dying? Maybe sharing it with the world would be the right thing to do. And Thexie. Well, she *would* make a good mother. As she sang, hands placed gently on her belly, swaying as if she were rocking a child, I imagined her singing a lullaby, a loving man by her side. I imagined a grandchild for Dad. Mother coming back.

From down below, there was a smash followed by screams. Sure enough, Captain Whoever and his crew had succumbed. We stopped singing, and applause erupted as the three visitors and Dad emerged from their hiding spot.

"Two thumbs up!" said Twyla. Phone bowed.

"Soooo sexy!" said Vince, and Thexie blew him a kiss.

"Incredible," said Kris.

I tried to think of a Daily Affirmation that involved accepting compliments but couldn't. I stood to the side as everyone whoop-whooped, cheered, and high-fived one another. My own father fist bumped Twyla Hoop. The level of tackiness hit a ten.

"I'm literally speechless," said Twyla. "*Snag-a-Siren* is going to be the biggest thing since *Glee*."

"I hate to be the party pooper," said Kris, once everyone calmed down. "But there'd be no more of this, you know, killing, once we enter negotiations, right? I think we can all agree it would be a PR nightmare."

My feeble family agreed. *Of course. Yeah, that would be a given. No more dead sailors, we promise.*

I opened my mouth to protest when Thexie chirped: "Here's to the last death song!" She raised her empty hand as if proposing a toast. "Here's to the future."

I slunk back to the house alone, ate five spanakopita and a bowl of yogurt with honey while standing at the sink. On the little shelf by the window there was a Happy Equinox card from Aunt Persephone. Beside it was the flute Cousin Pan gave Dad as a joke one Christmas (everyone teased him for being the least musical person in the family). On the shelf above that sat the bottle of 600-year-old mead Uncle Dionysus wanted to crack with us the next time he passed by the island.

I couldn't let all this happen. Someone had to stand up for traditional Greek values. For history. For all that my father had taught me. I started on a pan of baklava. Who were they kidding? Not even B-list celebrities were going to rush in to our dusty little piece of rock in the middle of nowhere. Phone wasn't going to get signed to some kind of multi-million dollar recording contract. People weren't going to watch another same-same reality show just for a lousy "date." Even if a Siren Sister was the booty. The whole concept was an insult to everything mythological. My family had stars in their eyes, preventing them from seeing properly.

I went into the washroom to puke everything up and it occurred to me that between permits and zoning and union shit, it would probably take years to get approval. And us *mortal*? Aging one year per year? At that rate, we'd be wrinkly, fat and grey in no time. Or — hang on — maybe we'd age one year per *boat* that went past. At that rate we'd be dead before the show aired. Shit, we'd be dead by Christmas! I had to save my family from their own weaknesses and vanities.

I gargled some Listerine, then crept past the garden party in the meadow. Phone and Thexie were too busy being seduced by strangers to consider going down to check for survivors from the wreck or to see what might have reached the beach. Vince was massaging Thexie's shoulders, and her eyes were half closed. Twyla was telling Phone something about royalties, the lucrative tween market, and hiring a manager. Kris had pulled out photographs of his grandchildren to show Dad.

"Dad?" I said. "Wanna come with me? Check what kinda loot washed up?"

"Thanks, Pins. You're on your own this time. Think I'm gonna just show our visitors around the island. Give them a taste of Siren family hospitality." Thinking back, I swear he winked at me, but at the time I just chalked it up to a twitch in his right eye.

I tromped down the cliff stairs to the wreckage. There were no fishermen's bodies ashore. Must have all sunk. The broken upper section of the boat, along with a cute old-fashioned wooden steering wheel, a couple of life jackets, and a piece of plywood were spinning in an eddy around Scissors Rock. Nothing salvageable had washed up yet. It could take days. Then again, if the proposal went ahead, there would be no need for us to scavenge food, equipment, home furnishings, or hardware anymore.

I sat for a long time on a flipped-over life boat and ran through my mental rolodex for an appropriate affirmation.

No. 4: *I am surrounded by people who love and support me.*

Nope.

No. 5: *When I feel overwhelmed, I simply breathe, repeat the serenity prayer, and let the emotions wash over me.*

Nope. The affirmations were pissing me off.

When I saw the Zodiac, I shut my eyes. I inhaled to the depths of my lungs, opened my mouth, and started doing what I did best.

Mother came back for Dad's funeral. The three other funerals were held in Athens, Italy, and the USA respectively. Mother brought her new husband Toshi-san with her, plus her stepgrandson Yusuke-chan. The kid fussed through the whole ceremony — until Thexie picked him up and coochy-cooed him quiet.

And now I'm the one my sisters can't forgive. I wasn't even singing loudly. Just loudly enough, I guess, for them to be enchanted. My sisters say Dad should have known better than to take Kris, Vince, and Twyla out in the Zodiac. I know in my heart that he *did* know better. He *let* it happen. He knew where I would be. Dad and I were the only ones who saw that the proposal was absurd. It was exciting to consider, but in reality it was a dream that would never fly. To accept their offer would have meant putting an end to a legend we've worked so hard to maintain. Dad and I saw the best way out. Phone and Thexie won't stay mad at me forever. There will be other sailors to pull out of the sea. Maybe we can put Phone's music up on YouTube or something.

No. 19: *I am not a number on the scale or a dress size or an age, I am the embodiment of spirit, and spirit lives forever.*

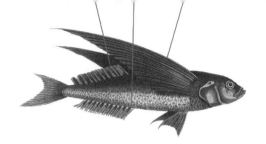

Mabel and Arnie

June 1

Dear Mabel,

You win. I get it. You've made your point. You wear the pants around here. There. I know how much it means to you to hear me grovelling. Fine. I'll beg, if that's what it takes for you to realize where you belong. Where your responsibilities lie.

I almost broke my neck climbing on the kitchen chair to take down the blasted smoke detector. Thing is so sensitive a man can't even fry an egg without getting the whole fire department out. One of the fellows laughed at that fridge magnet you've got: *Think like a Man, Act like a Lady, Work like a Dog.* Why don't you take your own advice? I wonder how "ladylike" Mr. Fireman would think it is for a wife to leave her husband and go off gallivanting for days on end?

Enough is enough.

Arnie

⌒⌒

June 2

Dear Sweetheart,

Linda stopped by but I didn't invite her in. I told her you were in the bath. She said it wasn't like you to have a bath before lunch and I told her you weren't feeling yourself. Lord, that woman pokes around more than a rat in a Chinese restaurant.

Mabel, when you come home, we should have a party. Invite Sara and what's-his-name. And little Kayla. You can make sandwiches. We could renew our vows like they do on television. Then we could go on a second honeymoon. How about Banff? (Maybe this time we'll leave the hotel room, ha ha.) Or that mountain in Africa or India you're always talking about. Darling, I want to marry you all over again. Please, Mabel. Give me another chance.

Linda said bridge was going to be at Anne's house this week.

XO, Arnie

June 3

M,

Someone telephoned. It was for you. A man. He was a foreigner. Spanish. Or maybe Pakistani. He said it was just a courtesy call. Anyhow, I told him I didn't know when you'd return the call and he said that was fine, he'd try again later. What should I tell him, this man, this *young foreigner*, when he calls back?

I don't even know when my own wife is going to be able to return a phone call to her lover. Can you imagine how that feels? Do you know what you're putting me through here?

Tortured,

Arnie

June 3, afternoon.

I've been thinking: I wonder what Kayla will think of her grandmother having an affair with some international "courtesy caller". For Pete's sake, Mabel. I guess the last fifty-seven years mean nothing to you. If you think you're getting another cent of MY pension, you have another think coming. Where's the bloody ginger ale?

From,

Arnie. (Your husband.)

❧

June 4, dawn

Dear Love of my Life:

I'm scared and lonely without you. I'm a useless, confused old man. Please, please, please come home. I'll do whatever you want. I'll stop drinking. I'll stop yelling. I'll be nice and gentle. I'll pitch in around the house. Dust. Polish the silverware. Whatever you want. I'll listen to you.

I woke up on the floor in the hall. I can't straighten out my right arm or turn my head at all. And I stubbed my toe on the chesterfield. Have you been moving the furniture? It doesn't matter. I don't want to die alone, Mabel, in a house full of traps.

Yours forever, Arnie

PS: We're out of milk.

❧

June 5

Dear M,

That Helen Weatherbee called. From Silver Spoons. I told her you were very busy these days and she wanted me to remind you that tomorrow is your day to lay the tables for afternoon tea at the senior's home. Your duties are at OUR home, Mabel. Here. With me. Not serving tea in fancy china to old fogies. Those dirty old men look at your backside, don't they? Do they grab your ASS Mabel? They are animals. I bet they paw you. I bet you like it. I bet you wear that yellow blouse. You really have stepped over the line this time.

Arnie

❧

June 6

Dear Peach,

I've stopped drinking. That's it. I'm on the wagon. Turned over a new leaf. (A dry one, ha ha). Trust me, I'm not doing it because I want to. I'm doing it for you. You always said you like me better sober. Well, here I am. Clean and sober. Since yesterday around noon. It wasn't a problem. Except for not sleeping a bloody wink. I can't find my slippers. My plantar warts are returning. I'm not complaining. I had water on my Grape-Nuts this morning and it wasn't that bad. In fact, it was hunky dory. I'm making positive changes, Mabel. Really, I am. I'm becoming a better man.

Love, Arnie

PS: We're out of 7 Up.

❧

June 7

Darling Mabel,

Linda stopped by again. She was downright snarly, not her usual irritatingly cheerful self. She said that your shiner is almost gone. Shiner?!? I didn't think it was that bad. Please tell me you're all right. I'm worried about you, my little turtle dove.

I don't know what turnip truck that snoop fell off of. Doesn't she know that all couples go through their ups and downs? You should be here with me. It's safe here, my plum. Haven't I always protected you?

Yours, Arnie

June 8

Mabel:

It's going from bad to worse. Tweetie's dead. There was a funny smell coming from the front room and then it all came back to me — the singing, those rubber gloves, the way you'd talk.

Why didn't you take Tweetie with you? I know. Your sister has a cat. Well, it doesn't matter. I never noticed how quiet a house can be, hearing aid or not.

I hope you're having a nice visit with Cicily. (I really do.) Please say hello to her from me. I am her favourite brother-in-law. What fun the four of us used to have, when Stanley was alive.

I've run out of socks.

Arnie.

June 9

Mabel,

I went into the tin. Sixty dollars? Are you kidding me? How long do you think a man can live on sixty dollars? Your allowance was $200 a month! That means you took $140 to your sister's. Are you hooting around town like a common hussy?

I also found your collection of newspaper articles. They were all yellow and old, so I threw them away. The Women's

Institute climbing Mount Kilimanjaro. A woman who ran a half-marathon at seventy-two years of age. Ridiculous.

Arnie

PS: The upstairs toilet overflowed because there was a houseplant in it — the African violet. You won't like all the buckets in the living room, but don't move them. They're catching the drips.

⌒⌣

June 10

Dear Mabel,

Sara called. Jeepers, she sounded cross. Did you tell her that her father is some kind of monster? She told me she was proud of you for being strong and taking a stand. "For once," she said. She told me I needed help and she was looking into extended care or some such nonsense. So I told her what's-his-name was a good-for-nothing layabout and that she and the kid would be better off without him. We need to have a serious talk about her. She's throwing her cotton-picking life away. I'm going to fix up her room for her so she can move back. Maybe put on a new coat of paint. Lavender. She loves lavender.

Arnie

PS: With a few ice cubes water is not as bad as you'd think. But still.

⌒⌣

June 11

Sweet Mabel,

I started ripping up the wall-to-wall today. It's a soggy mess. More "musty rose" than dusty rose, ha ha. Besides, it's poisonous. There are over 100 toxic chemicals in the average North American household. It was on *60 Minutes*. And your everyday carpet, plus the glue, is proven to cause cancer. Proven! We'll have a nice healthy wooden floor instead. Wooden floors are all the rage these days. What's old is new. That's what they say. If that's true, I must still have a price tag on me then eh?

I'll pick up a new pair of slippers for you from Zellers. Plain wood isn't nice to walk on. What size are your feet?

There was a casserole on the front steps. There was also a pamphlet from the Aspen Grove Seniors' Residence. That bum Sara's living with probably put her up to it. They'll toss me into an old fogey's home, sell the house, and use the money for marijuana and sports cars. The oven doesn't seem to be working, so I ate the whole thing cold.

It wasn't anything like one of your casseroles, Mabel. It might even have been vegetarian.

Truly,

Me.

❧

June 12

My Sweet Love,

Remember that night we stripped down to our skivvies and swam out to the big rock at Dragonfly Lake? It was a full moon, and we lay on that mossy rock. You lay your head on my chest and I thought my heart would explode. Bats were dive-bombing us and I asked if I could kiss you. You said, "Wait for the next shooting star." You've always made me jump through hoops for you, my love. Always! But it was August. Meteor season. So I knew I'd get lucky sooner or later. We stared and stared up at that sky, so starry it was like sand spilled on black velvet. And wouldn't you know it? Those goddamn stars just sat up there twinkling. Not a one shot across that sky. It must have been over an hour we lay out there. Freezing. Waiting. Wishing. But neither of us gave up, did we Mabel? And we never compromised. We lay there together, and talked of so many things. And laughed — oh, we laughed, just the two of us out there like a couple of giggling loons. And then, just before the hypothermia set in, as the sun was about to rise, a meteor like we'd never seen before streaked across the sky. It looked like your burning marshmallow at the campfire earlier. Its tail didn't burn out for one-one thousand, two-one thousand, three-one thousand, four-one thousand. We were necking by five-one thousand, and it felt like that meteor went right through me, Mabel. Do you remember? You told your folks we got a flat tire on the way home from the drive-in, even though your hair was soaking wet and it was practically morning. Oh, they didn't believe you one little bit. No, sir. They tried to keep us apart after that, but it didn't work, did it? Nothing can keep us apart, my love.

Forever yours, Arnie

June 13
Mabel:
Brandon McGregor, the neighbourhood extortionist and paper boy, is charging me an arm and a leg to pick these letters up when he delivers my *Sun* and take them to your sister's with her paper. Are you getting them? I don't trust that nincompoop and I don't want to be wasting one dollar per day to have him deliver these messages if you aren't even getting them. Please respond by letter or telephone. If I don't hear from you I will assume Brandon's an extortionist AND a thief.

Love Arnie

❧

June 14

Dear Honey-Pie,

Where did you put my jogging shoes? In case Linda stops by again I zipped to Barley 'n' Grapes. Ha! Zipped. Hardly. It felt pretty good to get a little fresh air. My slippers are now ruined from walking through that construction site. Next time I'll need my jogging shoes.

Love, Arnie

PS: Lipstick smudge at top of page is a kiss. Coral Moon certainly suits you better than it suits me, ha ha! But there you have it. The paper kiss.

❧

June 15

Dear Love of my Life,

Enclosed are a few of my hairs snipped off my head, around the back. Not many to spare these days, my dear, but I thought you'd like them to remind you of me. Sorry I have not been affectionate these past few years.

And a few fingernail trimmings too.

I miss you so much I get dizzy and it feels like my heart is a cold stone in my chest. It hurts, Mabel. Please come back.

Lonely, Arnie

❧

Mabel and Arnie

June 16

Dear Cunt:

I know you were at that stupid Spring Fling luncheon with Manfred York. How could you? Bitch bitch bitch bitch bitch bitch bitch bitch bitch bitch bitch bitch bitch bitch bitch! You can't stand him and the way he chews his food. That's what you always said. Did he talk to you about his model trains all afternoon? I just can't believe it. Why why why why why? I think I'm having another stroke. You've abandoned me for Manfred York, the cud-chewing model train moron, left me all alone in this cold house with no food or milk or money and no way to take care of myself. I'm dying of a broken heart and you are the slut who's broken it.

— A.

❧

June 17

Dearest Mabel,

I ate the last jar of pickled beets today. I remember how the house smelled so darn good during canning season. There's a package of pork chops in the fridge I'm saving for when you come home. I'm also saving some spuds I found in the pantry. And a head of lettuce. You just give me a little warning and I'll light candles, put Frank on the turntable. I'm sure Cicily appreciates your being there, helping her get over Stanley. You are a good sister. You are a rare gem.

I've put together a special care package for you. Tokens of my love, everything straight from my heart.

Love, Arnie

PS: Some girl came over today. Couldn't have been out of her teens. Called herself a Geriatric In-Home Caregiver something-or-other. Smarty-pants. I showed her the door of course.

❧

To Mr. Vortch: here's the package you wanted me to deliver yesterday. Mrs. Vortch says she wishes you would leave the family photos in their frames on the walls where they belong and not send them to her. My dad says this isn't really supposed to be part of my job, but I don't mind. As long as I'm paid in advance. In cash.

— Brendan McGregor

❧

June 18

Dear Mabel,

The rain's coming down so hard. Reminds me of the day we were married. Do you remember? Your sister married Stanley in St. Agathe's the year before, but nothing so fancy for us! It was a fine day, and we decided to walk to Town Hall rather than take the tram. But then the clouds rolled in and it started to pour! Of course, we hadn't thought to bring umbrellas, such optimists we were. You held my jacket over your head and we dashed as quickly as we could. I can still hear your laughter, clear as if you were right beside me. What a soggy sight we must have been on our wedding day. The justice of the peace married us anyhow, with the assistant librarian from down the hall and that nice old woman who happened to be signing out some books as witnesses. Mildred. That was the old woman's name. She gave us a ten-dollatr bill. Ten dollars! She said we looked like we could use it to start our marriage off right. We couldn't believe our luck.

We have been blessed in this life, haven't we Mabel?

Your bridegroom, Arnie

June whatever

Mabel

Someone's been coming in. To the house. Did you leave your key somewhere? Did you give it to one of your boyfriends? Every night I lock the deadbolt, and still someone's been coming in. They finished the two bottles of wine I bought at Barley 'n' Grapes (for Linda). Spilled some on the kitchen floor too. Now I'll have to go out and get more. They're eating the bread and there's none left. Had to eat just mayonnaise spread on a tomato today. The last tomato. Tonight I'm sleeping with the shotgun.

Arnie

Tuesday???

Dear Mabel,

What is the matter with people these days, Mabel? Tried to go to the market in case Linda or Sara came over.

The Taylor's marigolds are in full bloom. There was some kind of construction going on. I wasn't sure which way the market was. All the new highfalutin developments and all the workers shouting. Never seen so many Chinese. Mabel, I didn't know where the dickens I was! Sat down near some bushes to rest the knees. Saw some kids playing. Little girls. Remember how Sara used to squirm and wriggle and splash when you'd bathe her? How she'd put those bubbles on her head? "Not in your eyes!" you'd tell her. "It'll sting! It'll sting!" I'd get one of the big fluffy pink towels and wrap her up and tell her she was just like a little Christmas present and toss her over my shoulder. "Daddy! Be Santa Claus!" she'd squeal. "Ho, ho, ho! Merry Christmas! What a heavy sack of toys I have this year!" I'd spin her around and flop her onto the bed, in a fit of giggles. Oh, but then once her head hit the door frame. I can still hear the thud. Do you remember how she cried? She had that little goose egg. We thought it might be a concussion. We sat together at her bedside; had to wake her up every hour that night to check her pupils.

Idiot cops. I don't understand what's wrong with society today, Mabel. No respect. Talked about me like I wasn't there. Like I was just some senile old bugger off the street. Even went through my wallet.

I'm going to have to go to the market and get something to eat. Tomorrow that's what I'll do.

Love, Arnie

⌒

June . . .

Dear Mabs,

So here it is. I knew you'd want it. Not many left now! Put it under your pillow, wife-of-mine. Whatever the tooth fairy brings you owe me half. Ha ha!

Love, Arnie

PS: When is your trip over?

⌒

To Mr. Vortch: Mrs. Vortch wanted me to make sure you got this sandwich and these bananas. Please leave an extra dollar with the rest of the money you owe me.

Thank you.

Brendan McGregor.

❧

Today

Mabel,

Have my glasses. Don't need them. Nothing in the world worth seeing when you are not here.

Forever, Arnie.

❧

To Mrs. Vortch: the sandwich and the bananas and stuff were still in Mr. Vortch's mailbox. Also there was no letter to deliver to you yesterday or today. My dad said I should tell you. I didn't think it was a super big deal. But my dad said.

Brendan McGregor

❧

August 25

Dear Brendan,

Thank you very much for your support and kindness through this summer. Indeed, it has been an extremely difficult time. Mr. Vortch always spoke very highly of you as well. I know he appreciated your prompt and reliable service.

By the way Brendan, you may want to knock on the door where Mr. Vortch and I used to live over on Willow Avenue after school begins. The renovations are now complete and I believe the new owners will be moving in at the beginning of September. And yes, you're right: it will be strange to see different people there. For many, many years our home burst with joy and laughter and love. I have so many fond memories of those times.

In any case, I am sure whoever they are they will want to subscribe to the *Sun*.

Also, thank you for the beautiful going away card! What a talented artist you are. I certainly hope Mount Kilimanjaro is as beautiful in real life as you've drawn it.

I will telephone the Subscription department as soon as my sister and I return from our trek, to resume our home delivery. If you have time in your busy schedule, perhaps you would like to stop by and look at our photographs.

Sincerely,

Mrs. Mabel Vortch.

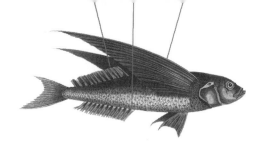

Swimming to Johnny Depp

THE NATTERING VOICES OF CHILDREN DIGGING for snacks and goggles and dry towels, the incessant wheeze of a debarked wiener dog tied to a picnic table, the shrieks of bikinied teens on an innertube splashing each other — it all fades to a dull hum when I see him.

Far across the rippling water, standing godlike on a raft floating in the middle of the lake, untouchable, sparkling in the sunlight.

On the dock I shake my head and rub my eyes. Could it be a mirage? A miracle? Heatstroke? He runs his fingers through his hair, and wipes the back of his hand across his forehead. Shifts his weight from hip to hip. Licks his lips.

I hear birds singing. Exotic birds. Extinct exotic birds. And some harp music.

The distance between us is an eternity yet it is nothing. His body glistens — tanned and dripping wet. He has the sleek muscles and taut skin of a racehorse. I don't need my glasses to know that it's Johnny Depp. Without that French girl. There's a Tibetan mastiff by his side. A glass of Chardonnay in one hand, a strawberry in the other. His hair cascades to his shoulders, oh, the shoulders of a man who could hold me tenderly one moment and build a set of shelves the next, shelves for his collection of literary classics and tastefully framed photos of his mother.

Did I mention that he's naked as a peach? Oh yes, my friend. I squint to see his nipples, pink as eraser heads, at 11:00 and 1:00.

And at 6:00 . . .

"What's that?" I mouth. "Who, me?"

He's motioning something. I look behind me, then back across the water to him. He's pointing. At me. Gesturing with his finger. Nodding slowly. His gaze pierces my soul. I completely forget that I'm holding a half-peeled hard-boiled egg in one hand. Warm liquid squirts through the straw of the juice box in my other hand and dribbles onto my foot. Understanding washes over me like syrup over a waffle.

He wants me to join him on the raft.

"Come alone," he whispers. The wind carries his words to me. I'm sure of it.

Mom! Mom! Where's my boogie board! Mom! Scotty's hogging the boogie board! Mom! Mom! Josh ate all the chips! Don't push! Mom! He's pushing me! Hey! Hey! That was my egg!

It's staggering how much one can block out when the love of one's life is beckoning, naked, from across a mountain lake. Staggering.

I step tenderly out of my Birkenstocks, point my arms over my head and dive in. I don't know how to dive. My belly, triceps, and thighs hit the water simultaneously with an ear-splitting thwack.

I am unfazed.

In fact, the burning sensation makes me feel alive. The sting-slap of lust vibrates through me. I surface and grab the ladder and catch my breath.

Mom? I hear faintly. *Mom? Are you okay? Scotty, look! Mom's in the water with all her clothes on!*

My senses are keen, my lungs fully oxygenated. I feel like I'm forty again. I take my hairband out and tilt my head back, throat to the sky. I can swim! I can swim to my love!

"Yes!" I sing out, exhilarated, shaking my hair above the cool, clear water. The teens hang on their tube, silently watching me. The wiener dog looks up, drops a flip flop from his mouth. An egg bobs beside me.

"Here I come, my darling!"

I bend my knees and get ready to push away from the dock and bullet through the water like a trout. A dolphin. An electric eel.

But wait.

From here in this medium of life, this liquid of love, I see him even more clearly. Waving at me. My Johnny is an impatient man. He's signalling for me to undress.

"Down to your skivvies," he says to the wind.

I am a woman hypnotized, entranced.

One arm wrapped around the wet wooden ladder like it's a pole on a burlesque stage, I undo the belt and take my cargo shorts off underwater, twirl them around overhead and toss them onto the dock. They land with a thump and I am vaguely aware that my keys, my phone, my prescription refill, my bank card, some bug spray, and a pack of Clorets are in the pockets. I pull my tank top off. And my socks. The cool water against my Jockeys For Her is invigorating. I realize that I'm wearing an old maternity bra, but it means nothing to me. Johnny Depp won't care. We have a deeper connection.

I thrust myself away from the dock, into the deep, cold lake. My body rockets forward. Front crawl or breast stroke? My arms part in front of my body like twin petals of a flower blossoming in the sun. I close my eyes and experience complete immersion.

They told me later it was a good thing I was wearing such a sturdy bra. Gave the Newfie-dog something to clamp his teeth on when he pulled me out onto the shore.

"Swear to God, lady, you were, like, blue."

"It was freaky, Mom."

"Yeah, and weeds came out of your mouth!"

"Holy crap. I've never seen anything sink so fast!"

Someone found my glasses under the dock, one arm broken off but otherwise fine. The swimmer's itch only lasted a few days. The kids refused to go back to the lake with me for the rest of the summer. Johnny Depp must have returned to the south of France, and I know Tibetan mastiffs get mistaken for Newfies all the time.

In the meantime, I'm taking swimming lessons at the community pool and my instructor is this stocky, blond, blue-eyed Brad Pitt-type who seems to have a thing for older women.

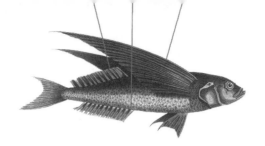

Bounty

I LEAN THE WET CROSSBOW AGAINST the wall outside the door and tiptoe into my old bedroom. I don't want to wake up Warren or little Maisy, so I say the words "ever so quietly, ever so quietly" in my head. It helps me focus on not making a peep — no easy task in these clumpy boots, which, come to think of it, I should have taken off on the porch. Oops. I drop my gloves and those good-for-nothing HotShots hand-warmers on the dresser beside our wedding photo. (Jesus, was I ever skinny! Both of us. Charles and Diana we were, back then. People even said so.) I clasp my hands together like I'm praying, just to keep them from shaking. I'm breathing like Dave's old dog Shep, so I stop. But that kind of hurts so after about five seconds I start panting again.

Jagged light from the hall shows me where not to step: Maisy's Groovy Girls tent trailer, Brenda's yoga bag, Warren's jeans.

I've got the spare room downstairs now, which is very comfortable. I can get out hunting early without waking a soul. I've got all the amenities a man could ask for. My own TV, a closet big enough for a foosball table, and a bathroom that no one uses but me, which I keep tidy and only flush when I feel like it.

"Brenda," I whisper on an inhale, without touching her. "Brenda. Wake up."

My wife looks like an angel when she sleeps. A princess. She has this honest-to-goodness glow, like she's fluorescent. Or lunar. I want to lift her out of bed and swing her around the room. There would be music. Sparkles would fall from her hair. I want her to follow me outside and run her fingers through the smooth hair of the beast, look at me tenderly, her hands clutched under her chin, and call me her hero. Blink slowly and tell me I'm legendary. I want her to see the trail of blood through the snow and say that she's never seen anything like it, except in fairy tales, of course, where the magical powers of certain animals is well-documented. I want her to cancel her and Warren's plans and spend the day scraping the skin to prepare it for drying.

Dr. Rivers says it's good that I'm learning a new skill. She says anything that gives my life purpose, meaning, and structure is part of the healing process.

I tell her that the whole "healing process" thing tends to backfire on the unicorn, which must be dead to be of any use to humans.

She says it's good that I have retained my sense of humour. Everyone agrees that a sense of humour will speed up my recovery.

Brenda lies at the edge of the bed, one arm dangling over, lips parted like the petals of a blooming rose. Maisy starfishes most of the space between her and Warren. She must have crept into their bed while I was in the woods. (Good thing we got a king size!) Her pudgy arm is against Warren's back; he's smushed against the wall. Their skin — hers and Warren's — is exactly the same colour. I've never known a grown man so pale.

People say he could be her father. People crack me up.

Poor guy barely has any covers. He's bone thin and must be freezing. It's 6:25. He likes to read the paper and have a leisurely coffee, black. The whole family agrees he makes the best pancakes in the land.

But not yet. This morning flapjacks will have to wait.

"Honey. Get up." I gently shake her shoulder. She's wearing my old "Think Fast, Hippie" T-shirt. My knees crackle like dry pine in a fire as I squat down, my mouth level with hers. She didn't used to snore, back when we were first married. That I would have remembered.

Maisy rarely stays where she falls asleep. She wanders, groggy and puffy, out of her room and crawls into our big bed for a cuddle almost every night. Dr. Rivers asks me how it feels for me when my five-year-old snuggles up to her mother and another man.

"I don't think of it like that," I tell her.

"But that's what happens, is it not?"

"Sure. Yeah, that's what happens. There's no 'how do I feel about it,' it's just what happens because their room's closest. What's she going to do, walk all the way downstairs to me in the spare room? She loves that big old king bed. Besides, she does come into the spare room some mornings to snuggle with me. Mostly when Brenda and Warren's door is locked. So that's nice."

I don't want Maisy to wake up now because I know I look horrifying. My face is striped with thick black coal lines so I can wait among the shadows of the cedar and hemlock trees in the forest out back. Ted from the Buck Stops Here says to just use a piece of coal from the wood stove. Works as good as anything you can buy, he says. On my head is a black knit cap, and I smell like synthetic urine from a spray bottle. Ted said they can't tell the difference between the man-made and the real piss. My jacket and pants are smeared with a blood so rare it will hurt to do laundry.

I can't remember exactly when Warren moved in. Sometime after the accident, but I don't know if I was still in the hospital or in rehab or what. Now I can't imagine him not being here. He's got this laugh that sounds like a teenage girl. I tickle him in the ribs just to hear it. "Uncle Warren" they call him at Maisy's school. It's a hoot. We look nothing alike.

"Dude, how the fuck can you let that asshole move in with you?" says my buddy Dave Havner. "You know what we should do?"

"No, Dave," I say patiently. "What should we do?"

"We should pound his fuckin' head in, that's what we should do," he says. "You're — what's the word? — cockheld," he says. "Pussywhipped and cockheld."

Dave means well, but to be honest he doesn't come by the house much anymore, even though he lives next door and old Shep wanders over whenever we light up the barbecue. He says the whole situation makes him feel uncomfortable. Actually, he said it was sick and twisted, but I understand what he was getting at.

Warren says Dave has a negative energy. I've never given much thought to Dave's energy. We still play darts most Tuesdays at the Thunderbird. No one needs much energy for darts. Dr. Rivers says it's good to maintain old friendships, maintain relationships with people from before the accident.

Brenda opens one eye. Wrinkles her nose. Opens the other one. Tries to get me in focus.

"Hey, sweetheart," she says, her breath like a fruit basket. "You're back early. Everything okay?" They're usually finishing breakfast and getting Maisy ready for kindergarten by the time I come back from hunting empty-handed. But this time it's different. This time I get to be a hero.

"I got one," I whisper, grinning hard.

"Yeah, right," she says with a smirk. She rolls over and pulls the covers over her head. I knew she wouldn't believe me; that makes it even sweeter. Inside, I'm bouncing.

"No. Really. Just before the creek past Havner's place. You've gotta come out and see. I dragged it all the way back."

She rolls back. Raises her eyebrows and props herself up on one elbow.

"Seriously?"

"Seriously!" I don't tell her what colour it is. Not yet. Or that it has a small spiral horn on its forehead. She definitely won't believe that until she sees it. She'll be happy the arrow punctured the chest and not the side so the hide will be clean. She'll have to see it for herself.

She swings her legs out of bed and scratches her head. Pulls the duvet up over Maisy and Warren. "Okay, let's go check out our venison."

Dave says my time in the hospital changed me. "Man, did that head injury turn you gay or something?" he asked once, on account of Warren. "I know guys had head injuries and they came out forgetful and kind of off-kilter. But not fuckin' queer."

"If I was gay you'd be the first one to know, honeybuns," I said, air-kissing him. Truth is, Warren moving in put the happily ever after back into our marriage. Brenda says she feels like the luckiest woman in the world. Warren's happy because he doesn't have to deal with someone wanting to have kids. (According to him, it was all his last girlfriend ever talked about and that was the main reason they broke up.) Maisy has someone new for hide-and-seek and I get to go hunting in the morning while someone else makes pancakes and coffee.

I wonder if unicorn meat will make good jerky.

I wonder how it will stew.

I wonder how exactly to process the horn and whether it will help with my memory and get me back on kilter.

Brenda steps into her Sorels, pinches her housecoat tight at the neck.

"It's cold," I tell her. "Put this on." I help her into my puffy jacket, bend down, and zip her up. She's so small it seems to swallow her.

"I can't believe you actually shot a deer," she says and pushes her hair behind her ears.

She opens the side door. Everything's the colour of bruises. I can't see the stars anymore.

A coyote cries and I feel panic rise. It rises into my throat and suddenly I know I have to tell her.

"Stop." I block the doorway like a drawbridge. "Wait."

"C'mon. Move out of the way, fatso." She tries to push around me.

Everything's going around and around, like I'm stuck in a flushing toilet. "No. You can't." What if there is some kind of punishment? Banishment? What if she screams and Maisy wakes up?

Dr. Rivers sometimes talks about breathing. I can't remember what she says about it.

"What do you mean 'I can't?' It's your first deer. You've been trying for months. Let's go."

I'm shivering. My tongue feels like a fist. I think I might vomit. "Brenda. You have to know."

"Know what?"

"It's not a deer. The animal. It's not really a deer."

"What are you talking about?"

"What I shot. It wasn't a deer."

"Of course it was a deer. What the hell else would it be? A brontosaurus?"

Footsteps. Our heads snap around.

"Hey," the shadow calls. It's Dave. "Saw the light on. You guys seen Shep? I heard him barking at something earlier but now I can't find him nowhere and I gotta go to work."

Shep never moves quickly, and you can feel the tumours when you pat him. Sometimes he wobbles into the woods at night but never goes far. He used to be white; now he's what Dave calls dirty blonde. In moonlight he still looks pretty white to me.

"Not here," says Brenda in her other voice. "If you don't mind, Dave, we're having a moment."

He comes closer anyways and sees the blood on me. "Holy shit, dude! You bagged one! Way to go, Ted Nugent! Big rock star hunter!"

I look down at my clothes, then it strikes me.

"So, you finally blasted Bambi!" he says.

What have I done? What have I done? It's not a deer. And it's not a unicorn either.

How can I tell him? He'll be devastated. Dave loved that mutt. A vision of Maisy when she was two riding Shep like a horse flashes into my mind. "Giddy-up, Sheppy-Shep!"

I pull off my toque and rub my face. Dammit. Dammit.

I'll tell him Warren did it.

No. I can't. He'll know, negative energy or not. He'll know it was me. Warren couldn't even lift a crossbow.

I grab the doorknob for steadiness, stare at Dave, and wipe my chin. I know this is what they call regression. It feels like quicksand.

"You look like shit," says Dave. "You gotta go lie down, buddy-o."

I step backwards, right into the coat rack. "Dave," I whisper. "I am so sorry. What can I say?"

"No worries. No worries," he says.

"No. Dave. Seriously. I think Warren killed your dog."

"What? Shep?"

Brenda flings her arms over her head. Her mouth bursts open but she doesn't scream. Her luminescent glow has faded completely away.

"Dude, what the fuck are you talking about?" says Dave, his head twitching to one side, standing up taller, hands on his hips.

"I don't know," I tell them. "It was dark. I don't know."

Brenda heaves a sigh. She gives Dave this look. He shakes his head. She takes my hands in hers and lifts them to her chest.

"Listen," she says, not angry. "Warren didn't kill Shep. Don't be ridiculous."

I yank away. Dave's standing over by the fence, whistling for his dog.

Oh God oh God oh God.

Whistling and calling to the purple forest and the world caving in and wouldn't you know it? Shep lopes out from under a bush, wagging his stupid matted tail like nothing ever happened.

"See?" says Brenda quietly. "You just got confused, baby. Shep's fine. You are a hunter. You killed a deer. I'm proud of you. It's gonna feed our big family."

She really believes this. She sees the goodness.

The storm in my head begins to settle. My fists unclench. She holds my face and kisses my closed eyes.

"Hey, lovebirds," calls Warren from down the hall.

"He shot a deer!" says Brenda.

"Actually, it's—" and I take my wife's hand and slowly lead her around to the back of the house.

Dr. Rivers says it's remarkable. She says in the last six months I've made tremendous progress. Another round of tests and an MRI and she says I may be ready to go back to work. The dizzy spells have stopped and I've lost fifteen pounds. I'm thinking much more clearly, and I'm doing yoga with Brenda every day. Sometimes the four of us play Fish or Crazy Eights in my room because it's cooler down there.

I'm not hunting anymore; I'd rather tend to the sweet peas and the Swiss chard in the garden. Dave married a waitress from the Thunderbird in June, and Maisy got to be flower girl. He even invited Warren, who looks much better now that he's sporting a bit of a tan. The skin of last winter's miracle bounty hangs on the wall on a diagonal that Brenda says is *feng shui*. Every morning Maisy climbs up on the back of the loveseat and strokes the bristly fur while Brenda and Warren are still sleeping. She hums as she pats it, and the stars on her PJs seem to glitter. There's enough meat in the freezer to last until Christmas, and I've found that by mixing powdered horn into the maple syrup, no one can even taste it.

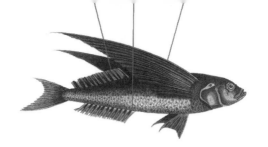

Your Best Interests

REST ASSURED YOUNG MAN. YOUR PARENTS always have your best interests at heart. Always. Your health, wealth, and joy was — is! — their number one priority. And they know that a quality education is the foundation. Wise folks, your mother and father.

Now. Have a seat while I review some of the changes with you.

Wipe your nose.

Oh, not on your sleeve. What are you now? Five? Use a tissue.

Where was I? Ah, your parents. Good people. They know their priorities. They know the meaning of the word "sacrifice". When it comes down to it, they know the Academy of the Refined Mind is simply a better school than the one you were assigned to by the Federal Department of Education. What was it called? Oak Street Elementary or some such thing.

Another tissue?

Of course, had you enrolled at Oak Street Elementary, a publicly funded institution, your parents' finances would not have been an issue.

But you? You deserve better. Your parents want you to be special. That's why they registered you here, choosing health, wealth, and joy over sick, broke, and depressed. And we know that they will have no regrets, don't we? Let's see ... it says here you were on our waiting list for twenty-one months before you were born. That's what I call Planned Parenthood. It's not your fault their dreams outpaced their personal finances. Sometimes things just happen.

Sit up straight, young man.

Shoulders back.

That's it. We don't want to appear to be a sloucher now, do we?

Did I mention that this is for your own good?

We don't train our teachers in Switzerland and Japan, with methods based on educational research developed over the past seventy years, combining elements of successful pedagogical models from dozens of nations — especially Scandinavian ones — for *nothing*. Students of the Academy are guaranteed to excel.

Is there something outside the window that is distracting you?

I know this is a great deal to digest.

Pull the curtains behind you closed, please. Yes, you may stand on a chair. There now, hop down.

Shouldn't be much longer. There is just a bit of paperwork to complete first. Feeling nervous? "Thou think'st 'tis much that this contentious storm, invades us to the skin" is it? Worry not, young man. Soon you will be happily translating Latin into French, mapping the stars, redefining pi, and interpreting Rilke. How could your parents not be excited about the possibilities for your future?

Ah, yes. The future. Our *raison d'être*. Academy of the Refined Mind alumni achieve intellectual superiority early in life, thus ensuring many years of health, wealth and joy. In fact, one of our eighth grade students — sorry, can't name names yet — was scooped up by a multinational finance company and will soon be earning six figures *per month*! See? Wealth and joy. Two out of three before adolescence. You'll read about it online soon enough.

Fingers out of your mouth, please, young man. We don't do that here.

I always tell people: "gifted" doesn't mean free. It's only through rigorous educational training that health, wealth, and joy can be achieved. And what parents don't want their offspring to be fit, rich, and happy?

Which brings us to the cold truth that financial hardships are a reality. Indeed, the current downturn in the economy has affected everyone, even some families here at our school.

Your parents undoubtedly entertained the possibility of enrolling you in public education — we recognize that tuition for quality schooling is not insignificant. Both faculty and administration here are relieved that they didn't take what we call "the easy way." Joining the masses is never the answer. Why, if you were at Oak Street Elementary, this year's cutbacks in government funding would see you and your peers hawking cheap chocolates door to door or selling tickets for a chance to throw a ball and drop the principal into a dunk tank. Preparation for a life of — what? — fast food sales and gambling? The humiliation of elders?

Besides, your parents will receive a substantial percentage of your income when the time comes. That's written into the deal.

I'm sorry, what's that?

You are mumbling.

Why of course they love you. Haven't you been paying attention? They will *always* love you.

Listen. For centuries, proud parents have done what is necessary to ensure a better life — the best life! — for their offspring. It is the root of our great nation's entrepreneurial spirit. Consider yourself part of a tradition of fortune seekers. Our mandate is to facilitate such a tradition through our unique fundraising events. For your parents' contribution to our "October Auction," you should be eternally grateful. Without the foresight, and yes, *love*, of people like your parents, last night's auction would not have been possible.

Oh dear. What's that smell? Do you need to use the washroom?

Are you sure?

Well, let me know.

And not to worry, you will most certainly see them again. At some point. The Winter-mas Concert is just a few months away. They are more than welcome to attend. And there's the Annual Medieval Festival in May. We invite the entire community to this joyous gathering, and there's always someone who tries jousting against Mr. Tribnor. Perhaps this year your father will be the one to take up the challenge. You could see him then! Cheer him on!

But the important thing is this: thanks to your parents, the Academy's funding requirements for your tuition have now been met (and then some!). Soon, you'll be able to pursue your academics *pas de problème*. It has always been our philosophy that consistency in the classroom can compensate for whatever changes occur at your home. Or, *to* your home in this case. Don't think for even a moment that your education will be adversely affected here at the Academy just because you were auctioned off.

Your new parents are obviously in a very solid financial position. They have assured us that your family reassignment will be as fluid as possible.

So, you see? There's nothing to be upset about. Chin up.

Pardon me? Yes, of course you have to call them Mum and Dad. That is part of the package.

Now, for heaven's sake, don't scratch your head.

Why are you scratching your head like that? Don't tell me your scalp is itchy.

That's the last thing we need. Here. Let me have a peek. Come over to the light. It hasn't been itchy for long, has it? I have a nit comb in my desk. Stay right there. Okay. Sit still.

Jesus. Where are my glasses? Why today?

You haven't been playing with those Fenton boys from Oak Street have you?

A bit closer. Quit moving. I don't see anything.

It's probably just dandruff. You have dry skin, right? Tell your new parents that you have a spot of dandruff. If they ask. You've probably had it for years. Everybody has a bit of dandruff. It's quite inconsequential. And that would explain the itch. It's more of a tingling sensation than an actual itch, right? Lots of children have dry scalp.

Here. Comb it back into place. Smooth down that side. Okay. That's better.

Pardon?

Oh, you are a funny one. My dear, with the amount of money they spent, I don't think that *liking you* is going to be an issue. They perused your pre-auction material last week, and are very much looking forward to taking you home today.

You are a charming young man. Worth every penny. In fact, we haven't seen a bidding war like that since those darling Vogler twins were auctioned off a few years ago.

Besides, with the way the stock market is going, there may be a need for the Academy to hold another student auction next semester. I can think of several other less fortunate but equally visionary families who would benefit from a slight shift in family arrangements.

In fact — and I shouldn't be telling you this — your new parents have expressed their desire to diversify; perhaps invest in a second child, if all goes well after today. A sister perhaps? So there's something to look forward to. It might even be one of your new classmates. Wouldn't that be fun?

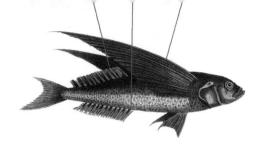

Suburban Wolf

From across the parking lot, no one can tell us apart. Except Steele, who's obvious, by his giant shoulders and how he stands with his legs so wide. And Amber, by how she slants towards Steele. Our hoodies — including mine — are like dark blue snowy fur glowing under the streetlight. We all sneer the same way. I look carefully at Steele to be sure. We look hungry and bored, which we actually aren't. Well, a bit bored.

"Carry on, pigs. Carry on," Steele growls. Sometimes it's like that; you don't give them the finger or leap on the hood of their car or throw rocks at them or run when you see them and they just leave you alone. After a bit, the cruiser does carry on, slowly. Driver's side cop catches my eye. I accidentally smile, so Steele tunes me with the back of his hand.

"Dickhead," he calls me.

"Sorry, man. Sorry."

Amber's lip curls up, her teeth catch the orange light, lip rings sparkle. Her eyes are big and sad like a cartoon deer's, almost covered by her bangs. I look away, warm. Stupid.

"Fucking right," says Steele — not to me — as the cruiser bumps out of the lot. "Off ya go." We all "uh-huh." One of

Steele's eyelids twitches in the cold, but I'm probably the only one who notices. My left eyelid feels twitchy too.

It's my birthday today but I haven't told anyone. Maybe that's why I'm making eye contact with cops and looking too long at Amber. It's not that I'm thinking of cake and presents and my parents and that kind of bullshit, but everything is magnified when it's your birthday. Like you have a twenty in your pocket and no one else knows. Or someone left pizza in the fridge and you find it. Or you have new socks on.

Steele hucks the empty spray paint can at a stop sign. Totally misses. It hits a fence. A dog starts going ape-shit. Amber laughs. Oona does too, until Amber doesn't.

I say there might be more spray paint in my uncle's garage. He locks it at night but I know where he keeps the key and there might also be fireworks in there from Halloween that we could help ourselves to.

"Shut up, Wagg," Steele says. "Go get me some smokes."

Crazy Mack comes with me, as the decoy. Makes like he's going to pocket a Mars bar. Old Man Chang screams some shit and waves his arms.

"Hey! Whoa! Take it easy, old man!" says Crazy Mack. He puts the chocolate bar back on the rack and lifts both hands in the air to show that he's clean and has no weapon and I creep under the front counter and lift two packs. "Relax, dude!" says Mack. "I's just lookin'. Don't have a fuckin' hernia."

Steele cheers up after his first cancer stick, so we go drop rocks through the book return slot at the library. There's a shopping cart behind the recycling bin at the mall. We push it into the creek. I'm thinking how next year on my birthday I'll look back and go, "Oh yeah, I remember what I did last year. Cool." And today will be a good memory.

At the cemetery we try to kick over headstones. We stomp on the lame ones that are just markers on the ground. We find a family plot: the McKinnons. Names and years and plastic flowers and a bench. "Must have been rich," says Crazy Mack, "to get a bench." Danny says he wants to be cremated and his ashes put into a taco and served to his stepdad. I'm about to crack up but Steele doesn't think it's funny.

"This kid was only four when she died," says Oona pointing to a ceramic angel. "Check it out. And this guy here was over one hundred. Magnus McKinnon. Guy saw three centuries." Danny argues that that's not possible and Oona tries to explain it to him. Steele takes a piss over Ethel McKinnon's grave.

"I'm fifteen today," I whisper to Amber, lying by a year, and smiling so hard I almost feel my ears move back.

"You're what?" she says dreamily. "Fifteen? You mean it's your birthday today?" Her mouth hangs open and her eyes juice up like she's never heard of anyone having a birthday.

"It's not that big a deal," I say. "It's just another fuckin' day."

"Hey you guys!" Amber squeals. "Guess what! It's Wagg's birthday!" Everyone looks at me. Even Steele. I am the centre of attention. I just nod and frown like I'm listening to music and really into it. Oona claps her hands and someone cheers a bit.

Then Amber takes my face in both hands. "You are the most *adorable* birthday boy *ever!*" she says slowly. "Happy birthday, Wagg!" And she comes at me with this wide open mouth and presses it over mine. I'm shocked and scared and can't breathe. Her eyes are closed, her head tilted almost flat sideways, and she's moaning. She tastes like fruity gum. Across her shoulder I see a diagonal version of her official-for-four-months boyfriend. Steele's shaking himself dry, zipping up. I can't see his face exactly but from the red glow of his smoke I know he's looking this way. I try to pull away but her hand grabs the back of my head. It's not like I've never made out with anyone before, but there's too much spit and I don't know what to do with my mouth. Or my hands. I don't want to be rude so I open wider. She's practically eating me, licking me and kind of chewing, poking her tongue around. A wad of gum is in my mouth now. I shut my eyes. She loves me. She must. I feel like a shooting star, blazing across the sky. Everything is wet. Salty. Slippery. I think my nose is dripping and I'm hard as a mickey in my jeans. I lift up my arms to put them around her.

Then I open my eyes and see Steele lurching towards me through the cemetery. My face drops away from hers. I'm done for. Dead meat. Headstones and trees start spinning around and I taste those fries coming back up. I may as well just lie down right here with the McKinnons. It's all over.

"Let's get out of here," says Steele. He takes Amber's arm gently and says, "This is boring."

"Damn right," says Oona quietly.

Amber wipes her mouth on her sleeve. I let mine stay wet. It starts to freeze like that and makes my boner last longer. The snow swirls and falls on me and Steele and everybody like confetti on a parade.

"Hey, stud," says Crazy Mack when Steele and Amber are out of earshot. He knuckle bumps me. I don't raise my hand too high up for him. In case she sees.

We head back across the lumber yard and into Fernwood Acres to snatch Christmas wreaths off people's doors. We throw them like holiday Frisbees down the street. Most bounce and roll in the orange glow. One made with real tree branches explodes when it lands. There's this one made out of fake apples and fake cinnamon sticks Oona says she wants to keep, but Steele wings it onto the elementary school roof.

I've got a plastic Frosty the Snowman. From the Stoddart's front yard. It's almost my size.

"Birthday Boy carries it," Crazy Mack says, and fair's fair. We sprint across Highway Nine to drop it off the overpass, but the road's slippery as shit. I go down hard.

Crack my elbow, crack my head.

"Fuck! Wagg!" cries Amber, letting go of Steele's hand and running towards me.

Headlights blaze across her face. She freezes, lit up, arms spread like a snow angel standing. Driver lays on the horn. Car misses her, barely, fishtails slow-mo into the ditch, flips on its roof.

Everything is still for a moment, hanging like it's not real, like a curtain dropped in front of the real world. The only thing moving are the car wheels, which keep going around. There's a whistling noise and creaking. Some smoke, or maybe just drifting snow. But I think smoke.

Amber's face is pale as milk and her lips are almost blue. She's shaking. I take her cold hand in mine and we get to the other side where everyone's huddled together like a pack of wolves in a grove of trees. They pull Amber in, rub her back. Oona tells her it's going to be okay and smooths her hair over and over. Then they let me in. We're all out of breath. Leaning on each other. Someone pats my back too.

"Holy shit," says Danny. "I thought you guys were roadkill." He looks at my head. "You look fucking gross, dude."

I touch my forehead. It's wet and stings. It hurts way more when I see the blood on my hands. My elbow aches. I suck it up.

Oona dabs at my blood with her sleeve pulled over her hand.

A couple of cars drive by but nobody stops.

We're waiting for Steele to say we should get the hell out of there before the cops come. Instead, he lights one up, all calm and silent. He offers me a drag. Even holds it while I inhale.

"Sorry," I croak. I am closer to his face than I've ever been before. He must shave every single day. His eyes are speckled with gold. He shrugs his enormous shoulders and lays one finger gently on my lips.

"Yeah. It's all your fault. Happy birthday, little asshole."

Then Amber tips her head into his armpit and the two of them walk through the snow, up the ditch, and along the side of the highway towards town.

He doesn't say, "Let's go." He doesn't even look back.

Oona says we should go over and check if buddy's okay. She grabs Crazy Mack and they start to head over there, but I say "No. Don't," and they stop. "Stay here. We gotta stay together. Cops'll be here soon." They both come back into the circle. She presses her shoulder against mine and we all stand shivering in that grove of trees, snow falling like it's nothing, and wait to see if the car will blow up.

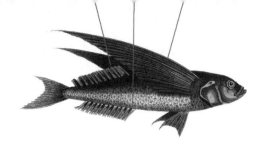

Scratching Silver Linings

MIKE, A SKINNY, FRECKLED NINE-YEAR-OLD WITH crusty eyes and buck teeth, stood facing backwards on the karate club's Canada Day float as it cruised down Frontier Street, his arms folded across his chest, serious as a national anthem. Beside him, kids did barefooted high kicks, chopped imaginary piles of bricks, and shouted joyful *hi-yas!* at the crowd of halter-topped girls, cowboy-hatted men, and sticky children.

The float itself was no more than a ribbon-festooned flatbed trailer hitched to Wayne Sensei's old Chevy. But being in a real live parade was no trivial affair for Mike, who would not permit even an inchworm of a smile to crawl across his face that morning. Not only was he patriotic, he was also terrified he might fall off. Eight fat Shriners giddily circled their tiny cars in the Chevy's exhaust, and Mike was sure that should he fall, their little tires would run over him repeatedly.

Beyond the Shriners' maroon fezzes with their swinging yellow tassels was the Only-A-Loonie Store's float, upon which his mother Petunia and two other jiggling, bikini-clad women romped in a large plastic kiddie wading pool. He watched them flipping their bleached hair this way and that and spraying the crowd with water pistols.

Mike's dream was to one day to walk in the parade, perhaps with some exotic animals. They only allowed certain people to do that. That would be a big deal.

"Hey! Mikey! Heads up, babycakes!" Petunia screamed and directed her spray towards him. The pistol wasn't powerful enough to squirt past the Shriners, and Old Man McQuade — a potato farmer who, at eighty-two years old, still wove his tractor through the fields from spring until fall and grumbled every Friday night to the bartender at the Legion about how the low-carb fad was killing business — got soaked. Old Man McQuade shook one crooked finger at Petunia, honked his miniature car horn with the other hand and hit a pothole, nearly pitching the little car ass over engine. This sent Petunia and her friends into a fresh froth of laughter.

Mike's focus was unbroken. He did not smile, and he did not duck when a Shoppers Drug Mart frisbee flew in his direction.

"It's gonna hit me? It's gonna miss me? It's gonna hit me?"

The disc clonked him square in the face. Blood gushed from his nose onto his karate uniform, just above the white belt. Petunia dropped her watergun and jumped off the still-moving Only-A-Loonie Store's float. She wove between Shriners and hoisted her bleeding son off the karate float.

Wayne Sensei continued to chug along, his hand waving out the truck window, unaware of the drama unfolding behind him.

"Why didn't you duck?" asked Petunia as she marched him to the first aid tent behind the library. "I know you saw it coming."

Ed Knee, the first aid volunteer, told Mike it must be his lucky day to get a bloodstain in the shape of a maple leaf. "Today of all days!" said Ed Knee. "You should buy a lottery ticket!"

Mike couldn't see the maple leaf. "It just looks like a plain old bloodstain to me."

"Oh, don't listen to him," said Petunia. "He's always been the glass-half-empty type. Looks for the cloud behind every silver lining. Just like his father." She reached across Ed Knee for some fresh Kleenex and whispered. "My ex."

Once the bleeding finally stopped, Petunia took Mike to his dad's condo. "Kid's got to lay low, Ian. Do you think you can handle that?" His dad was a mechanic and always seemed to be covered in a thin layer of motor oil. They were both skinny and freckled. Ian said he would do his best.

That night Petunia watched the fireworks in Centennial Park with Ed Knee. They sat shoulder to shoulder on a black-and-red checkered picnic blanket. ("He's so upbeat!" she told her girlfriends the next morning.)

Mike and his father watched the fireworks from Ian's back deck overlooking the park, but went inside before the grand finale. There was a tear on Ian's greasy cheek and a bandage on Mike's nose.

Mike was a sullen fourteen-year-old with stringy black hair and a face like a butter tart with braces the next time he was in the parade. He plodded behind the 4-H club, shovelling what was left by the llamas, ponies, pigs, and sheep that other kids his age had hand-raised on their farms. In front of them, Petunia, slightly lumpier but no less perky, spun and twirled and shimmied in a dress made of bandanas and leather strips with the local chapter of the Wild Thyme Dancers.

Mike's dream was to one day be a parade organizer, shut off certain streets to traffic for the special morning, know the whole route in advance. That would really be something.

Someone on the sidewalk blew a tin noisemaker too close to the marching menagerie. One of the 4-H piglets got spooked, broke her leash, and darted away like a first grader at the recess bell. Mike saw the squealing weaner heading straight for him as he was about to rake a particularly large pile of llama manure into his dustbin.

"She's gonna hit me? She's gonna miss me? She's gonna hit me?"

The pig knocked his legs out from under him. He buckled, twisted in the air, then dropped. His dustbin and rake landed on the sidewalk a few metres in front of him.

"Why didn't you just step out of the way?" asked Petunia on the way to the clinic. "I know you saw that pig coming. You can move faster than some little farm animal, can't you? You didn't even try! You've got to start trying."

Dr. Dumas said it was pure heavenly luck that the llama dung cushioned Mike's fall and prevented his head injury and twisted knee from being more serious. "Saved by the *merde!*" said the doctor, his arms outstretched. "Hallelujah, my friend. You have a guardian angel. You should buy a lottery ticket!"

Still, Mike didn't feel lucky. While he changed out of his poop-covered clothes, Petunia chatted with Dr. Dumas ("Call me Pierre") about fate and dancing and raising teenagers. Dr. Dumas said he liked her eyes and her teeth and invited her to the cafeteria to share a poutine.

That night, Pierre and Petunia watched the fireworks from a paddleboat in the middle of Clearwater Lake. ("He doesn't like crowds," she told her girlfriends the next morning.)

Mike was kept overnight in the hospital for observation. The nurse brought an extra fruit cup when his dad showed up. His dad stayed and they watched the fireworks broadcast live from Ottawa on a small TV screen, then channel surfed for three hours until explosions from local celebrations shook the walls and startled them both.

When Mike was sixteen, he was in bed for most of the summer with a moderate case of mono that he'd picked up after accidentally using his cousin's toothbrush. He lost almost fifteen pounds but his mother said there would be no point in buying him new clothes, even though his old ones no longer fit.

By seventeen, he'd put the weight back on (and then some). On Canada Day weekend, he went RV camping at Alice Lake with his father but it rained non-stop from Friday until Monday and they pretty much didn't leave the Holiday Rambler.

At nineteen, he had a job as a night cleaner at the movie theatre. He cleaned up spilled pop and squished popcorn until 3:30 AM. He slept until late afternoon every day that summer in his room in his mother's basement. By mid-August his complexion was that of a garlic clove.

He was twenty-one the next time he was part of the Canada Day parade. As Assistant Traffic Patroller stationed at the intersection of Frontier and Arbutus, he wore a reflective vest over a white T-shirt, diligent khaki shorts, and sunglasses. He felt the uniform lent him an air of dignity, despite the sweat that streamed down the sides of his face. It was his responsibility to prevent cars from mistakenly turning onto the parade route. For this, he had a technique and two tools. He could signal the car away with his hands, or if that failed, he could blow his whistle and hold up a stop sign.

The job spurred thoughts of directing traffic at intersections when the power goes out and the lights don't work or even at car accidents. A bona fide, full-time, paid traffic cop. That would be something special.

Petunia, wearing demin short shorts and a red tube top, the kind that does not make allowances for a brassiere, bounced exuberantly along the parade route distributing paper flags and temporary tattoos to spectators. She tried to get him to put a maple leaf tattoo on his cheek ("C'mon Mikey, it'll be so cute!") but because he was in uniform and on the job, he firmly refused.

A heavy heat wafted above the pavement and cloaked the marching bands, Boy Scouts and Girl Guides, decorated donkeys, and convertibles full of waving dignitaries and top realtors. People on the sidewalk fanned themselves with takeout menus they had been given by Dragon Pearl Express Chinese food restaurant. Everyone sighed in relief when the occasional gust of wind swept down the street.

It was during one such gust that Mike noticed something pink or red — a scrap of paper? — spinning in the air in front of a monster truck.

He watched the rectangular scrap rise, fall to the street, and lift again, carried towards his post on the street corner by the summer breeze.

"It's coming to me? It's not coming to me? It's coming to me?"

The paper landed silently above the radio pocket of his reflective vest, stuck to his body by the wind. It was a fifty. He looked around. He fully expected someone, perhaps its rightful owner (but perhaps not), to grab the bill off his chest.

His brow deeply corrugated, Mike examined the bill. He flipped it from the politician's picture on one side to the snowy owl on the other and back again. It looked new.

Wow. Why would a fifty-dollar bill, more money than he was expecting to earn for his whole morning as Assistant Traffic Controller, appear out of thin air and settle right there on his vest?

Slowly it dawned on him that his luck might be changing.

Perhaps destiny was smiling upon him and it was time for him to smile back.

Without notifying the head traffic controller, he left his post at the intersection of Frontier and Arbutus and skipped to the 7-Eleven where he purchased forty-seven dollars worth of Scratch & Win tickets and a large Slurpee.

It was reckless.

It was thirst quenching.

And it felt good.

During Mike's absence, a rented CanaDream RV driven by a confused German tourist mistakenly turned onto Frontier Street and drove into the back of the Lincoln convertible carrying honourary parade marshal Roberta Bondar, Canada's first female astronaut. No one was injured, but the parade was delayed for twenty-five minutes. Old Man McQuade and his fellow Shriners made themselves sick with dizziness driving around and around in one spot while they waited to get going again.

When Mike returned to his post, Steve Stock, a bald, thick-armed tow truck driver with a hairy back, white plastic sunglasses, and a dirty purple tank top, was hitching up the damaged Lincoln to haul it to Kirk and Mel's Autobody. (The RV did not appear to have suffered; the German couple was doing an extensive visual scan.) Mike unenthusiastically waved the rest of the parade around them while Petunia applied a fake maple leaf tattoo to each of Steve Stock's biceps, holding the saliva-moistened decals in place slightly longer than was necessary. ("He's so big and strong," she would tell her girlfriends the next morning.)

Mike was disconsolate. He wanted to run away, but he did not. Instead, he waited for the parade to unsnarl, then he claimed sunstroke, handed back his vest, stop sign, and whistle (the sunglasses, T-shirt, and shorts were his own) and went to the beer gardens in Centennial Park where he sipped two pints of beer over the afternoon.

It was almost dark when he remembered the lottery tickets he'd stuffed into the side pocket of his shorts. He pulled them out, but before he started scratching them, the German couple from the CanaDream RV asked if they could share his picnic table.

"Sure," he said as they slid next to him. "Why not."

"Vat a vonderful celebration. Ve vere so lucky to end up in dis village today of all days," said the man. "Ve couldn't have asked for better bad luck!" said the woman. They both laughed and ordered a pitcher.

Mike nodded, flipping the tickets with his thumb like they were a deck of cards.

Petunia, Steve Stock, and Ian (who worked at Kirk and Mel's Autobody and had watched hockey with Steve Stock at the Legion more than once) appeared.

"So this is what you spend your wages on, eh?" said Petunia, eyeing the lottery tickets.

"Well? They aren't going to scratch themselves, are they?" His dad pulled a coin from his pocket and handed it to Mike. "Use this. It's my lucky penny."

Mike, who had never known his father to be a superstitious man, began scratching the silver lining, uncovering the words *Try Again!* and *Better Luck Next Time!* ticket after ticket after ticket.

There was moaning and groaning and hands slapping on foreheads after each losing ticket was revealed. No one could believe it. "Lucky my ass," said Ian, taking the penny back. The Germans laughed. Steve Stock said it was some kind of crazy warped luck to not win a single thing out of forty-seven tries. "Not even a free ticket! It's a friggin' miracle is what it is. Against all odds."

Petunia stroked the tow truck driver's muscular shoulder, shook her head, and said, "I knew it."

It dawned on Mike that it really was against all odds. Maybe he was blessed.

"Oh well, what never was can't be lost," said Steve Stock. "And by the way, buddy, if you're in the job market, I've got an in with this crew that does traffic control. You know, at accident sites and whatnot. It's year-round. As a rookie, they'd have you working all the holiday shifts. It's always a bugger to find guys willing to work long weekends. I could hook you up."

Mike smiled. It was all coming together. He tried to respond, but fireworks drowned out his words. "I'll call you," mouthed Steve Stock. He did the signal for talking on the phone with his thumb and pinky at the side of his head, then put his arm around Petunia's waist. The Germans poured beer for everyone. His dad placed a greasy hand on Mike's shoulder and all their heads angled skyward as elaborate explosions lit up their faces, over and over and over.

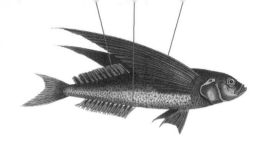

Representing Literature in Music for You

FIRST OF ALL, NO MORE MR. Williamson. It's Mr. W from now on. In fact, why don't we drop the formalities altogether? You can just call me Paul. Okay? Welcome to off-campus class at Tim's! Wave to the staff. Good. Hopefully you guys all did your homework. We don't have a lot of time, so get your coffee and donuts and whatever and let's get going. Gonna be a super-exciting class. Trey, what song did you choose?

"Spank Me Before You Leave".

Okay. Coolio. Thanks. So. Before we look at the video, can you tell us what it is about this song that represents literature in music for you?

I don't know.

Well, what's the song about?

It's rap.

And why did you choose it?

It's good?

Okay. Let's take a listen. Turn your computer so everyone can see. Travis, can you see? Trenton? Bring your chairs closer. Oh. Yeah. They're attached. Well, just gather round. Troy, stand where you can see.

(5 secs)

193

Hang on. Crank the volume up so we can hear it over the muzak. Must be a bank robbery somewhere in town, eh guys? No cops in a Tim's? Right?

(4 mins 32 secs)

Yeah. So. That was good. Now, can you tell us why you like that song?

I already did.

Can you be more specific?

Um, because it's about people that grew up and one guy leaves and the rest stay at home partying and then the guy died.

Wow. Yeah. Sad. That's really sad.

I guess.

Do you think it's a social commentary? Is there a universal message here?

What?

Do you think it relates to your own life?

It seems true.

Does it make you think of your childhood? The friends you may have lost touch with? The mistakes you may have made along the way? Regrets?

What?

You know, regrets. God knows, we've all done something we wished we hadn't. Don't get me started on regrets.

Not me.

Listen, I know you're only in eleventh grade —

I'm in twelfth.

Okay, eleventh and twelfth, but you're all coming from different backgrounds and you have different goals and I respect that. We all take different paths in life, and we've all got something valuable to say. That's what makes this class valuable.

It's the kind of class I wish I could have had when I was in school. Back in the day. But hey. Clock's a-tickin'. Let's move on to Tristan. Tristan? Are you ready? Have we lost Tristan? Where is Tristan?

He went out for a smoke.

Okay. Travis then. Are you ready?

I can't connect.

Did you enter the password?

Password?

timhortonsriverside

Oh yeah.

Now. Do you have a song for us?

Yup.

And? What's it called?

"Fat Chance Road".

Awesome. Okay. So, why this song? How does this song represent literature in music for you?

I like the beat.

Okay. Good point! Rhythm in language is much like rhythm in music. Think of iambic pentameter. It's really another version of 4/4 time. Do you think maybe Shakespeare was the first rap artist?

And it, like, talks about different things.

Fantastic. Are there any lyrics that stand out to you? Anything that really resonates? You know, gets you in the gut. Speaks to your soul.

Dude spent the night in a drainage ditch dreaming of doing home renos.

Interesting. Let's have a listen.

(3 mins 55 secs)

Okay. Sure. What do you guys get from that song?

It's cool.

Can you expand?

What?

Anyone? No? Well, okay. Here's my two cents. I think it does offer some social commentary. The guy's looking at all the things he didn't do. It's saying how you can try and spruce a place up by putting on a new coat of paint, but you can't make up for missed chances. I think it's referring to all the things he should have done differently when he had the chance. Maybe he's stuck in a job he doesn't really like. He really wants to make a difference. Maybe he dreams of being a writer. Maybe freelance. Getting a publishing contract. Or maybe he wants to be a musician. Maybe he plays a little guitar, can find his way around a harmonica, maybe his folk band got a few gigs, but then they broke up and who knows if they ever would have hit the big time. I don't know. Nobody knows! People have all kinds of dreams and ambitions and they just set them aside because you've got to pay the rent, right? Your girlfriend gets pregnant and suddenly you're married, driving a minivan, struggling to make ends meet, trying to remember what your dreams were. But hey, I'm just the teacher. It's not about my opinion. I wanna hear from you. What do you guys think? Trenton? Trey? Troy? Tyler? Hmmm? What about you, Tristan? Tristan, you're soaking wet. Why are you soaking wet?

'Cause it's raining.

Oh.

My song's by Spit On It.

Okay. Sweet. I like S.O.I.

(25 secs)

This is stupid.

Trevor, let's not interrupt. It's his choice and you'll get a chance to share your opinion.

(15 secs)

It isn't even a song.

Tristan, pause the vid. Trevor. I'll give you the floor. Tell us. Share with the class why you think it's stupid.

It's just talking.

Okay. It's talking. So Trevor has issues with this song. Question: is it musical literature even though it's just talking? Anyone? Anyone? Does music require melody? Does talking require rhythm? Does poetry need rhyme? Does story need plot? Is there a character? Which comes first here, the story or the words? No? Okay, well, unpause it. Tristan?

My computer froze.

Really? All right, we can wait. Do you need to reboot?

No. Doesn't matter. He's right. It's a stupid song.

Hey, Tristan. Don't say that. It was your *choice.* Personally, I think it's got a pretty good message.

Whatever. Tyler can go.

Okay. That's up to you, Tristan. We're not going to force anyone to do anything here. Well, unless Principal Ray walks in, right? Ha ha. Then we're all in the crapper, right, guys? Gotta follow the *curriculum.* So. Tyler? What's your song?

"Screwed for the Ninety-Ninth Time".

Okay. Sounds great! Let's have a look-see.

(22 secs)

It's taking too long to load.

We'll wait. Tell us a bit about it.

It starts with a picture of the capital building. The one in Washington. Land of the dead-beat, home of the slave.

Wow. Tyler. I'm blown away. Is that from the song or did you think of that yourself? Mind if I use it some time? Just kidding.

Okay, here goes.

(3 mins 16 secs)

I can see some of you guys are nodding. So this is actually really interesting, right? I mean what is the message of this song? It's pretty inflammatory, right? Historical footage of riots. Pretty intense, eh? Rosa Parks? Martin Luther King? Shots of Uncle Sam with a turban? Do you think this is propaganda? Do you think this is literature? Is it politics? Is it a call for a revolution?

My friend has a beard like Uncle Sam.

Poverty. Depression. Drugs. This song has it all. Great choice, Tyler!

Does Canada have a Uncle Sam?

'An' Uncle Sam.

Look! I got a free donut.

What's that, Trey?

I rolled up the rim and I fucking won!

Hey, buddy, that's awesome. Congratulations!

Swear to God, I never win anything. I'm gonna go get my free donut. Maple dip. Maple dip rocks. Be right back. Nobody take my spot.

Okay. Let's carry on. So. Does this song strike a chord in you?

How much longer do we have?

About ten minutes. For me, it's interesting all right. I mean there's a pretty strong message in that song. Is it literature?

Possibly. Could you see people making a music video like this about Napoleon in *Animal Farm*? Hey? Hey?

They don't have Maple Dip. Fucking sold out. Fucking joke.

Aw, yeah? Too bad. Well—

Pisses me off. They make you buy a coffee and then they sucker you into unrolling the stupid rim. Like you have to actually dismantle a disposable cup.

Okay. Well —

It's humiliating.

Indeed. We should carry on —

Like we're all rats in a science lab. They wanna see how far we'll go doing a ridiculous task with a cheap cardboard cup in the hopes of a pathetic little reward. But at least the rat gets the cheese. Here, you achieve the so-called goal and you have this moment of holy shit! Life is good! You think you're pretty awesome. You imagine that maybe this is the change you've been waiting for all your life. Things are going to turn around 'cause you are the chosen one and the angels are smiling. And then the donut you want is sold out so you're shit outta luck. Again. They are actually laughing at you, the angels. Back to the start, loser rat.

Yeah. That sucks, Trey. Anyways, have a seat.

This is what keeps the lower class in a constant state of false hope. Needy and desperate. Suckers for a dream. It's what keeps government and big business alive.

Hey, can I do mine now, or what?

Sure, Trenton. I think Trey's through. What's your song?

"Thunder and Lightning".

They said take a Chocolate Dip instead of Maple Dip. It's bullshit. It isn't right. It's the tyranny of oppression. There's this perception of freedom of choice, but it's all just a grand, sugar-coated illusion. There is no choice. No justice. No hope.

Okay, Trey. Now. Let's carry on. Is there a video with "Fire and Rain", Trenton?

"Thunder and Lightning".

Right.

No. Just the song and this image.

Image?

Of rain.

I'm gonna go take a piss.

Okay, Trey. But please hurry, class is almost over.

(3 mins 12 secs)

Good. Great. What made you choose that song?

Rain, corn, whiskey.

Aha! Full circle. Social commentary? Life in the south? Addiction? Possibly. All right, cool. Music? Literature? Literal music? Anyone else? No?

Is this going to be on the exam?

No. It's almost time to wrap it up here. Where's Trey?

He's still in the washroom.

What's taking him so long?

Dunno.

So this is your homework, okay? Read chapter eight of your text.

You assigned that last week.

I did? Okay, just kidding. Read chapter nine. And here's your assignment for next class. Brainstorm your ideal society. What it would be like. How you would run the world. And include lyrics from a song. It can be from one of the songs we looked at today.

Or it doesn't have to be. Actually, no. You don't have to include lyrics. Just brainstorm your ideal society.

Do we have to write it down?

Yes. This is an essay assignment.

How long?

Five hundred words sound okay? Let's keep it around four or five hundred words. Include government and economy and social structure and law and all that.

I would be the dictator. You wanna be in my society? You have to do it my fuckin' way.

Yeah. No thanks. Screw off. I want my own society.

Ha! Good luck with that.

Sweet. Okay. Wow. I can already tell this is going to be really interesting. Good class, guys. Travis, could you go and get Trey? I don't want him to miss the assignment.

Sure.

And for the rest of you, here's the last thing I have for you before you go back to the school. Trent, pass these around.

What?

It's your essay prompts. Just to give you ideas about your ideal society. Don't lose these sheets, okay?

Do we have to use these ideas?

Yeah. Unless you can come up with your own. So head straight back to the school, okay? If you're not there in time for Chemistry, I'm the one who gets in trouble. Hey! Hang on. What the — is that Trey back there behind the counter? What's he doing? Trey, what are you eating?

Oh my God. That's hilarious. Dude, get out your phone.

On it.

This is great, Paul! "High School Student Loses it at Tim Horton's."

Okay, Travis. Shhhh. Stop filming. This isn't funny. Where is the staff?

I always knew buddy was psycho.

Trey. Trey. Listen, my friend. What are you doing? You need to come out of there. You aren't allowed back there. Put down those donuts and come back over the counter now, before someone calls the police.

This is going to get a million hits on YouTube! This is totally gonna go viral.

Okay, hop over. Yeah, that's it. Watch your leg. Jesus, that jar is for the kid's camp. Oh my God, Trey! You can't just scale the counter and help yourself to whatever you want at a restaurant!

Tim Horton's is hardly a restaurant, *Paul*.

Zip it, Tyler. This isn't about you. Now seriously, Trey. What the hell?

There were fresh ones on the rack. I saw them. Just out of the oven. I won one fair and square. I get my choice.

Shit. There's the manager. Do you think they're ever going to let us have off-campus class here again? Last thing I want is to have to explain this to Principal Ray.

They owed me one and I took it. Plus one for my inconvenience. I'm standing up for my civil rights.

Okay, the rest of you guys head back to school. Looks like I'm gonna have to deal with this.

It was my right as a free citizen.

Don't talk with your mouth full, Trey. You know what? Don't talk at all. I'm not interested in what you have to say anymore.

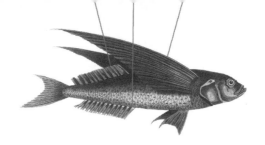

The Anniversary Present

MOTHER EARTH WAS HUFFING AND SNORTING in the kitchen, slamming cupboards and muttering to herself, things like *ungrateful crater* and *good-for-nothing swamp rat*.

Chunks of bleached hair lay like twisted wool against her sweaty, oatmeal-coloured skin. She'd recently had a microderm-abrasion treatment to invigorate her complexion, but her frown lines still looked as if they'd been etched by eagle talons; her eyes angry woodpecker holes, despite a new Puffiness Reduction Formula she'd been applying diligently.

She took the casserole out of the oven. It was burnt. She banged it on the stovetop and wiped her hands violently on her apron.

That was it.

"Do you have any idea what today is?" Her big bare feet pounded across the lino. The spices in the rack above the sink shuddered but Father Time had dozed off in the La-Z-Boy by the fireplace. He didn't even twitch. His mouth was wide open, a bead of drool perched on his beard. The book he'd been reading lay open on his chest.

"Faker!" Mother Earth whacked him across the head with an oven mitt. The old man sat up with a start and adjusted his glasses. Wiped his mouth. The book fell to the floor.

"I have been waiting all day. For you to even acknowledge it. For you to do something — anything — nice for me." She frowned and her thinly plucked eyebrows converged above her hefty nose. "I made you a special meal. I vacuumed. I shaved my goddamn legs!" She hurled a small green box at him. It hit him in the shoulder. "And you forgot."

Father Time rubbed his arm, gulped, and looked around the room. Where was he? Was it morning? What day was it?

"Sorry?"

"Happy anniversary, asshole." She picked up the book. It was an atlas. "And don't snoop through my stuff!"

Mother Earth stormed into the bathroom and locked the door.

Father Time looked at the calendar on the wall. March 21. Circled in red.

Right.

Shit shit shit.

He picked up the box she'd thrown. It was about the size of a pack of cigarettes. He held it to his ear and shook it gently. It had obviously been wrapped by one of those professional gift-wrapping services, with two different coloured ribbons, expertly curled, and the tape was practically invisible. At each end the paper was folded into a perfect triangle. She used to wrap things in leaves or seaweed. Tied them up with vines. She was more upscale now. He stuffed the gift into his cardigan pocket and lurched out of the chair.

How could he have forgotten? With work matters it was different. Years. Seasons. Days. The whole universe. Right down to the nanosecond. Why did he always seem to mess things up at home?

"Lover?" He pressed his ear to the bathroom door. "Lover? Open up. Please. Don't be mad."

The toilet flushed. It was her way of not letting him hear her cry. Even after all these years, she hated him to know how much he'd hurt her.

She gazed into the mirror and wiped wet mascara from under her eyes with a piece of toilet paper. There was something about watching herself cry that usually cheered her up. Not this time.

"Who are you, old hag?" she whispered. "What the hell happened?"

"I do have something special for you. I just have to wrap it," Father Time yelled. "And I can make us reservations somewhere nice."

"You are a bad liar and a bad husband."

She hurled the Skin-So-Slick towards his voice. It made a satisfying smash and cream dribbled down the door like moon milk on a cave wall.

Silence. The shuffling of feet.

A jumbo tube of Cleer-Cut Depilatory Cream hit the door just above the Skin-So-Slick. It bounced off and landed near her foot.

Mother Earth squinted at the mirror over the sink, at her yellow teeth, cracked and eroded from endless nights of grinding, and threw a box of Smile, Honey! Tooth-Whitening Kit, figuring that the little kit from Shoppers Drug Mart wouldn't be heavy enough to shatter the glass.

But hey! What's seven years' bad luck?

A bottle of Retrograde Metamorphism Serum mocked her from the shelf beside the shower. It had been formulated in a science lab. She'd spent a fortune on it. Each night she blended two to three drops in a circular motion under each eye until they were absorbed. She emptied the whole vial into her hand and slapped it on her face. She raked what was left on her palms through her hair, until it stood up. She looked like a grey sea anemone. She opened the medicine cabinet, on a roll now. There was that bottle of Faultless Beauty Vitamin Complex she'd bought from a perky redhead at Body Beautiful last year. That little tart had assured her she'd look and feel one year younger for every month she took the pills. She dumped about sixty into her hand, filled a glass with water, and gulped the years back, several at a time. She squeezed pineapple-scented PaleoTropix Body Butter onto her tongue. Couldn't hurt. Cream up the old insides too. She swallowed the oily goop and started feeling giddy.

Bring it on, baby. Gimme some of that good stuff. Creams, serums, gels, pills, sprays, vitamins. Mother Earth applied, snorted, drank, sprayed, and swallowed. Where was a hypodermic needle when you needed one?

"Lover?" asked Father Time. He heard banging and bashing, some wheezing, and the occasional grunt. "You okay in there?"

No answer.

He figured it wouldn't be long before she unlocked the door and came out with one hand on her ample hip and the other stretched in front of her and said, "Well? Where's my present, wise guy?" And when she did, he'd better be there with something good or he'd get the Arctic shoulder for a month of Christmases. He'd better haul his skinny arse into town and hit the mall.

Father Time tiptoed to the mud room, slid into his rubber boots, buttoned his cardigan, and put on his hat. The front porch was a disaster. He stepped over a pile of lumber scraps, three rusty coffee tins full of screws and loose change, a broken staple gun, the cordless drill, the skill saw, some crumpled blueprints, and a few empty beer bottles.

They'd been doing renos. She wanted an enclosed veranda. "We'll sit out there and not worry about the bugs or the rain, and we'll play board games and sip mint tea."

He shuffled down the driveway, past the wild blackberry bushes, the old apple trees, and the cherry tree. It seemed like only yesterday they'd argued about what to call that one. She'd wanted to call it the Love Tree. He'd wanted something more specific. They agreed on Cherry, and when it finally blossomed, they spent that whole afternoon rolling around under it, exploring each other, revelling in the product of their compromises. Just a couple of crazy kids, he thought, then stepped on a rotten cherry pecked to shreds by magpies.

Good grief, thought Father Time. Would this driveway ever end?

He turned around to see how far he'd come, and hoped to spot his wife at the front window, watching him from between the slats in the blinds. No luck. He sighed and soldiered on, dizzy from looking backwards. He was already pooped. At this pace it'd take a century to get into town. Unless he could hitch a ride. Yes, he'd put the old thumb to work.

He remembered her once saying something about couple's counselling. Together. Honestly, he didn't see the point. They'd been through thick and thin. Tectonic shifts and ice ages. The Industrial Revolution. The invention of asphalt. They'd get through this rough patch too. What good was a few gab sessions with an overpriced shrink going to do? People changed. People got older. Not everything went the way you planned. That's life. "This too shall pass," he was fond of telling her. "Easy for you to say," she'd respond, shutting him down like an eclipse. He kicked a stone in the driveway and it ricocheted off the fence. His hip ached like a bugger.

It had all seemed so easy back then. Effortless. When they were first married, he could make her smile with a fossil, a pearl, a calcified rose, some trinket that would mystify her. She'd hold it, fondle it, turn it over and over in her hands, rub it against her cheek.

"Did you make this, you crafty fellow?" she'd say, teasing. "I'll show you what else I can make," he'd say and grab for her and she'd giggle and they'd collapse in a tickling heap and she'd love the wind out of him and he'd be happy. Those were the days. If he could, he would loop time, but that was a trick only Hollywood had mastered.

He wasn't one to complain, but, truth be told, it wasn't just his hip. His back ached too. He didn't know if it was related, but he had been much more limber before she started nagging him about every little thing around the house. All these stupid makeovers and home improvement projects. It was never-ending. He'd considered asking her if she was going through the Change, but had thought better of it.

Whatever it was, she spent most days flipping between the Nature Channel and *Desperate Housewives*. Quoting Oprah and ordering things online. Accusing him of being old-fashioned, out-of-synch, uninspired.

What was a guy to do? He felt guilty about it, but how could he *not* fantasize about Sister Moon now and then? Even a man of his age had certain needs. She was so natural and innocent and pure. It lifted his spirits just to think of her luminescent skin, her radiance, her consistency. On nights when she was full he'd sometimes slip into a reverie and linger just a little longer in her presence, not willing to let her fade into the day. No one ever seemed to notice, except for the wolves and the criminally insane.

Finally, he reached the end of the driveway and leaned on the mailbox to catch his breath. He'd wait there for a car to come and take him into town. People were friendly in the country. You never had to worry about weirdos.

Mother Earth sat on the toilet, sweating, legs wide apart, head tipped back, opening capsules of Bioturbated Anti-Aging Pills one by one and sprinkling the phosphorescent powder into her eyes. Her heart was galloping. There was a tremor in her foot that would not stop and a cramp just under her left collarbone. Her nose was so congested she could only breathe through her mouth, which was as dry as an Alberta gopher hole. Empty bottles, vials, jars, and tubes littered the bathroom counter and the floor. There was a blob of yellow gel in the sink.

It wasn't just the forgotten anniversary. No, siree. It was his whole attitude. There was always some excuse. She wanted to go on a cruise. "Too claustrophobic," he said. She wanted to go to Europe. "Too expensive." She wanted to take ballroom dancing, pottery classes. "Too embarrassing. Too messy." She knew he felt redundant these days — not like before, when the calendars didn't even include July and August, and accuracy meant a sundial on a clear day. Back then, he was actually needed, respected, even honoured with festivals and the burning of goats. Now? He simply didn't have the power he used to. She knew it made him feel impotent. "You need something to look forward to," she'd told him. She tried to be sensitive to his emotions. She went to great lengths to make him feel special, ignite the passion in him. He was such an ungrateful old geyser.

There wasn't much left in the medicine cabinet now — just some expired homeopathic shit that didn't even give her a buzz.

She found a little Vibrant You Tonic under the sink between the hot water bottle and the curling iron, so she chug-a-lugged it, and chucked the empty bottle into the tub.

A capsule of Nannofossils lay on the floor. She pinched it open, held it under her right nostril, squeezed the left one shut, and sniffed hard. Immediately sneezed. Powder sprayed every-where. Mother Earth laughed hysterically.

A Smart Car zoomed by Father Time. Didn't even slow down. Oh well, no room anyhow — the passenger seat was full of recycling.

Next, a VW van approached. It was painted with peace signs, flowers, and a rainbow and was followed by a cloud of black exhaust. He stuck out his thumb and smiled, but the driver didn't see him. Probably stoned. Perhaps he should have called for a cab.

Not that he minded waiting. He needed the break. He could feel his heart beating hard against his ribs from the walk down the driveway. Maybe Mother Earth was right. Maybe he did need to get more exercise. Build up stamina. Get on a program with a personal trainer. That's what he'd do. And what the hell. He'd go to some marriage counselling with her. Take her on a cruise if it meant that much to her.

Happy wife, happy life.

A two-toned Morris Minor drove by. Was that Sinatra on the radio? Father Time held his breath and put one hand to his ear to catch the fading strains of "One For My Baby" as the car rounded the corner. Sure would have been nice to catch a ride in that, he thought.

A few minutes later, a Model T puttered up the road. Well, that was something you didn't see very often these days. Must be an antique car and truck show in town. Father Time waved as the shiny black car approached, but the driver didn't wave back. Do I really look that suspicious? he wondered, stroking his beard.

He lowered himself to the ground, stretched out his legs, and leaned against the mailbox post, sweating but too exhausted to take off his cardigan. Closing his eyes, he heard the rhythmic clip-clop of a horse's hooves, and the squeaky whine of the wooden buggy it was pulling.

So tired.

Just a little nap. Then he'd get himself to town, to the mall. Somehow.

Get that perfect gift.

Make it all better.

Sleepy.

Sleep.

"For external use only, my ass," Mother Earth mumbled, reading the warning label on the thin smoked glass bottle of Paradise Rapture Cologne, her hands trembling and her vision wonky. It had been hidden on his side of the bathroom cabinet, behind his deodorant and his shaving cream. She rarely even opened his side of the bathroom cabinet. Why would she? His shit, his mess.

She licked her chapped, swollen lips, and tossed back the velvety potion like it was a shot of tequila.

What's a little chemical intervention?

The bathroom went dim. Wow. The tiles seemed to be rotating.

It might be time to sit down, she thought, sliding down the wall as a rancid taste filled her mouth and a heat wave spread through her body.

Maybe that last bottle was a bit much.

Slowly, Mother Earth began to vibrate. The rumbling of a volcano. She belched long and loud, then lay her quivering body upon the cool bathroom floor.

She bumped her head on the toilet but felt no pain. Her heart slowed to a prehistoric thud and her thick eyelids sank peacefully shut.

When Father Time's eyes popped open, the sky was pink-yellow and the birds were singing. Son of a bitch! He must have slept by the road all night. His wife was going to be livid.

He'd have to admit that he had plumb forgotten their wedding anniversary, tell her he didn't have a present for her, admit to passing out on the mailbox, and kiss up to her for, oh, *ever*.

He stood up quickly, and with surprisingly little stiffness.

Something was different.

His hip. It didn't hurt any more. And his back. He reached both arms high into the air, and tipped his head from side to side as if to listen for tearing, cracking. No pain.

Father Time did a little boogie. "Hey, hey!" he cried. He hadn't felt this kind of energy since before the pyramids!

He looked around. A single red apple, a few cherries, and a scattering of blackberries. The driveway was overgrown with lush, thick grass, undulating in the wind. Up ahead, gigantic butterflies flew among yellow and purple and orange orchids taller than him. There was no mailbox. No fence, no telephone poles, no ditch, no road.

And, no house. Erased, just like that. He felt a catch in his throat. What happened to his wife? She was in there when he left. Then he saw movement, out by where the garage had been.

He took off his glasses and rubbed his eyes. Slowly, things came into focus.

There she was. Mother Earth, exactly as she had been on their wedding day, so long ago. Young. Vibrant. Radiant. She was laughing, her hair flowing behind her. And there was someone else. It looked like . . . could it be?

Sister Moon!

Father Time grabbed his chest. Miracles can make even an atheist thank God. Oh, yes. Glory be, there they were. Hand in hand, feet barely touching the ground. He heard songbirds he'd forgotten existed. He raised his hands to his face. His skin was as smooth as a peach.

"You-whoo!" Mother Earth called from across the meadow. "Hellooooo! Over here!"

Father Time walked on tiptoes toward them.

The way they were looking at each other — and touching each other — made him feel nervous. And excited.

"We have a favour to ask you," said Sister Moon.

"Just a teensy little one," said his lovely wife, without a hint of recognition.

"Lover!" He reached his arms out, dumbstruck. "Sweetheart! It's me!"

"It's so very nice to meet you," said Mother Earth, flashing him that flirty smile that made the backs of his knees feel like pudding. "If you aren't busy, would you mind just standing here for a while? Without going anywhere?"

He couldn't believe it. She was like one of those people on TV who goes into a coma and wakes up not remembering her husband or her family or what her favourite food is.

"My God," he whispered. "Don't you remember me?"

"Sorry," she said, hunching her shoulders up.

"But you do look like a great guy," said Sister Moon.

"So," said Mother Earth. "Do you mind?"

A huge purple and yellow bird squawked and swooped across the sky. This was definitely not the same world he'd left when he tried to hitchhike to the mall.

"Yes. I mean no. I mean, you want me to just stand here?"

"Keep an eye on the garden while we go exploring."

"A nature walk," said Sister Moon.

Peals of laughter.

What could he say? What else could he do? "Sure. Why not."

"C'mon, my love," said Sister Moon. The women wove arm through elbow and off they skipped.

"When will you be back?" Father Time called. "I could join you . . ."

But they were gone.

Confused, he put his hands in his cardigan pockets. The box. He pulled it out and turned it over in his hands. Slowly, he untied both ribbons, peeled back the green paper, opened the cardboard flaps, and pulled out a shiny black-and-silver stopwatch. Classic. Useful. The kind a swim coach or an official at a spelling bee would use.

He smiled and flipped it over a few times in his nimble fingers. I suppose this will come in handy while I wait, he thought. He pressed the Start button and waited for the *click, click click*. Nothing happened. He shook it and held it to his ear. Silence. Shook it again. Tapped the face. It needed a battery. There was a new package of AAA batteries in the kitchen junk drawer. He put the stopwatch back in his pocket.

"Happy Anniversary to you too," he said, looking across the meadow.

And with a long sigh, Father Time stood still.

Acknowledgements

"Cannonball" appeared in *FreeFall* magazine in 2010. A version of "Scratching Silver Linings" (previously titled "Lucky Mike") appeared in *Other Voices* in 2011. "Lunch Date" appeared in *subTerrain* in 2011. "Swimming to Johnny Depp" was published in the anthology *Never Light a Match in the Outhouse* (Summit Studios) in 2014. "Dire Consequences" was published in *Pique Newsmagazine* in 2014.

This collection would not have been possible without the support and encouragement of the Vicious Circle: Stella Harvey, Nancy Routley, Mary MacDonald, Sue Oakey, Rebecca Wood-Barrett, Libby McKeever, and Sara Leach. Thank you for enduring friendship and high standards. I am also deeply indebted to Zsuzsi Gartner, Brian Brett, Merilyn Simonds, and Fred Stenson for their incredible mentorship, to Michael Kenyon for bang-up editing, and to Tammy McIvor for moral support and tea. Special thanks to Jack and Lilah for your patience and inspiration. And to Bob, for love and kindness above all.

Photo by Anastasia Chomlack

Katherine Fawcett was born in Montreal, raised in Calgary, has lived in Japan, Yellowknife and Canmore, and is now based in Pemberton, BC with her husband and two children. She began her career as a sports reporter before venturing into freelance journalism and commercial writing. However, fiction proved far more interesting. Her award-winning short stories have been published in *WordWorks, Event, FreeFall, subTerrain* and *Other Voices*. She teaches music in Whistler, BC, plays the violin with the Sea to Sky Orchestra, and the fiddle whenever possible. *The Little Washer of Sorrows* is her first book of fiction. Katherine Fawcwett's website: www.katherinefawcett.com